DOPE GODS

Lock Down Publications and Ca$h
Presents
DOPE GODS
A Novel by *Hood Rich*

Lock Down Publications
P.O. Box 870494
Mesquite, Tx 75187

Visit our website @
www.lockdownpublications.com

Lock Down Publications
Like our page on Facebook: Lock Down Publications
@
www.facebook.com/lockdownpublications.ldp
Cover design and layout by: **Dynasty Cover Me**
Book interior design by: **Shawn Walker**
Edited by: **Lashonda Johnson**

Stay Connected with Us!

Text **LOCKDOWN** to 22828 to stay up-to-date with new releases, sneak peaks, contests and more…

Thank you.

Submission Guideline.

Submit the first three chapters of your completed manuscript to ldpsubmissions@gmail.com, subject line: Your book's title. The manuscript must be in a .doc file and sent as an attachment. Document should be in Times New Roman, double spaced and in size 12 font. Also, provide your synopsis and full contact information. If sending multiple submissions, they must each be in a separate email.

Have a story but no way to send it electronically? You can still submit to LDP/Ca$h Presents. Send in the first three chapters, written or typed, of your completed manuscript to:

LDP: Submissions Dept
Po Box 870494
Mesquite, Tx 75187

DO NOT send original manuscript. Must be a duplicate.

Provide your synopsis and a cover letter containing your full contact information.

Thanks for considering LDP and Ca$h Presents.

Hood Rich

Chapter 1

"Three hundred, four hundred, five, six, seven, eight, nine, a stack. Here go a gee. This is enough for your rent, right here. So, you should be all good." Javier slapped a rubber band around the remaining fifteen thousand he held in his hand just to stunt on Kelis.

Kelis was light-skinned, with hazel eyes, naturally curly hair, and had the body of a goddess. She watched Javier stuff the wad of cash back into his Marc Jacob jacket. Her hopes of getting more than one of her bills paid dissipated. "I'm saying Javier, I thought you were going to help me out more than that? I still have my car note, my phone bill, and a few others I need help with."

Javier stared at her slyly and licked his thick lips. Javier was five-feet-eight inches tall, Puerto Rican and Black, with short curly hair, and golden-colored skin. He was fit and took pride in his physical appearance. "I'm saying, Mami. I just gave you a gee. You texted me saying that my cousin, Peto was having a hard time helping you come up with the rent. Now I came over and helped you pay all that shit. You should be more grateful than what you are being." He looked at her across her living room table. Then stood up and headed toward the front door to her apartment.

Kelis jumped up and made haste to get in front of him. It was nearly impossible to get a hold of Javier. He was always outrunning the streets in either Miami or New York. After texting him back to back and hitting him up on Facebook she was finally able to convince him to come over so he could help her out. She didn't want to squander the moment with just getting her rent paid.

"Javier, please, can you stay for a little while? I need to tell you how hard things have been for me and Alexis ever since Peto stopped working for you."

"Peto didn't stop working for me. Peto got caught stealing, and if Peto wasn't my cousin, Peto would have gotten his head cut off. That's how shit is supposed to go." Javier felt his temper getting hot.

Peto had been skimming a few grams off at a time of each kilo that he handled at the traps Javier allowed him to run being that he was his blood. After catching Peto in the act by camera and beating him and the entire trap house full of workers senselessly, with the help of five other savages, Javier released him from his duties.

"I understand that, Javier, but there is no reason Alexis, and I should have to suffer. I mean I love Peto with all my heart but sometimes he can be a major fuck up. When he was working for you, we never needed for anything. Now, it's so hard to make ends meet. I just want the best life for Alexis. She shouldn't have to struggle like I had to growing up in La Perla. That's the reason I came here from Puerto Rico. I wanted her to have the best life, yet, here we are struggling harder here than we were there. It's not fair." She flipped her long curly hair over her back and ran her fingers through it.

Javier sized her up, she was so gorgeous to him. Though she was only eighteen she was mature and had a good head on her shoulders. She spoke with wisdom beyond her years. It sucked to him that she had wound up with Peto. "Kelis, how much do you love, Peto?"

"With all my heart, and soul. He is my husband. Our love is until death." She thought about Peto and felt fondly for him.

"Oh, yeah?" Javier pulled out five thousand dollars. He fanned it out so that she could see that it was all one-hundred-dollar bills. "You should never love no nigga that can't produce these. Fuck love, Bitch, love can't pay the bills. You understand me, right now?" He pulled her to him and cuffed her ass under the thin cotton nightgown with his right hand, while he held the money in his left.

Kelis fought her way out of his grasp and stepped back from him. "Javier what are you doing?" She blushed.

Javier took the money and held it up. "This is five thousand dollars, Kelis. Five bands." He turned and opened her front door just a crack, then turned back to her. "I wanna fuck you. I don't care that you are my cousin's wife. I wanna fuck you. In exchange for some of that pussy that I know is about to be fire, I'ma give you these five gees. And anytime you need me I will come to you. Can't another bitch in Miami say that."

Kelis backed away shaking her head. "No, Javier, I could never cheat on Peto. I've been with him since I was fifteen. I've never even thought about another man. He is my everything, despite his shortcomings at times."

Javier stepped into her face and backed her up until her back was against the wall. His lips brushed up against hers. "I don't give a fuck about none of that. We can do our thing, and you can still love your man. I ain't trying to take you away from him." He slipped his hand in between their bodies and rubbed up the center of Kelis' gown. He felt her thick pussy lips hidden inside the cloth of her panties. The feel and heat of her made him shiver.

Kelis felt like she was being watched by God. She tried to back away but found herself trapped by the wall. She placed her hands on Javier's shoulders. "Please, Javier, I can't."

Javier didn't like rejection. He was a boss, and bosses weren't supposed to be told no. He thrust his front into her and kissed her neck. "Kelis, Mamamita, you are a dime. You are supposed to be with a Boss. When you are as fine as you are you should never need or want for nothin'. I am here, I can supply you with everything you need." He sucked her neck and dropped the money at her feet. "That's yours, it's for you and Alexis." More sucking.

He slowly raised her gown with his fingers until it was around her waist. His fingers slipped back into her middle. He rubbed the front of her pussy packed panties.

"Javier, please don't." She tried to push him away, but her attempts were weak.

Javier slipped his hand into her panties and rubbed up and down her crease. Her lips were full of dew. He parted them with expertise and slipped his middle digit up her hole. She felt like a hot swamp. She gripped him and he tensed.

Kelis bucked her ass backward and removed Javier's finger from her pussy. She slipped out of his embrace. "Javier, you have to leave. Please." She ran her fingers through her hair, she was flushed.

She could feel her secretions running down her inner thighs. She hated herself for being so aroused, it was wrong. Javier was Peto's cousin, she loved Peto. He was her all.

Javier wasn't taking no for an answer. He snatched her up and pinned her to the wall. She shivered in his embrace. "Kelis, look at me. Look at me!" He held her by the shoulders.

Kelis looked into his eyes with her hazel ones. "I am looking at you, Javier. Now what?"

Javier searched her eyes with his own for a moment. He found himself trapped within hers. She appeared so vulnerable to him, so ripe for the picking. The fact that she was Peto's wife made things all the more alluring for him. He picked her up before she could prepare herself to be lifted from the ground. She wrapped her thighs around him. He sucked her neck and bit into it.

"Unnhhh! Stop, Javier. Please stop."

Javier fell to the floor with her on top of the hundred-dollar bills. He yanked up her gown, pulled her panties down her thighs, and off her ankles. He got between her legs rubbing her pussy. "You're wet, Kelis. This pussy is drooling. You want me. You wanna fuck with a Boss, keep that shit real. You're tired of fuckin' with a bum every single night. Aren't you?" He slipped two fingers up her pussy and slowly ran them in and out while his thumb played over her erect clitoris.

This technique was new to Kelis. She humped into his hand involuntarily before she caught herself. She tried to scoot backward, but Javier pulled her back to him. He lowered his face between her thighs while he held her sex lips open. He sucked her pearl into his mouth and flicked from side to side with his tongue. Kelis screamed and opened her thighs wide. She humped upward from the ground and tried to find the fight within herself to retreat from Javier.

"Javier, ooohhh, please."

Javier forced her knees to her chest. He took her whole gap in his mouth and slobbered over it. His tongue traced her crease hungrily. He sucked lightly on her clit and nipped at it with his teeth just right. Kelis screamed again. She bucked, trembled, and came hard digging her nails into his shoulder. Her cream squirted on the corner of his mouth and dripped off his chin. Javier continued to slurp, and suck until Kelis became so wet he knew she was ready for him. He got on to his knees and released his dick.

"Kelis, taste me mami."

Kelis felt herself oozing, she was so ashamed. "No, I can't."

Javier stroked his piece faster until it was rock hard. He brushed the head over her lips. "Come on, baby. Taste me, open up."

Kelis moved her head away from him. "No, Javier, you have to go. Please."

"Go?" Javier positioned himself back between her thighs and ran his piece up and down her slit. She was dripping wetter than ever. Her heat felt like a mouth breathing on him. He scooted forward and slipped into her pussy burying himself as deep as he could. It felt like he was sticking his piece into a hot bowl of soup. His eyes rolled into the back of his head, then he was fucking her like a savage with her left calf muscle on his shoulder.

"Uh! Uh! Uh! Javier! Oh, shit Papi!" She opened her mouth wide, struggling to breathe. She panted and swallowed her spit. Her nipples felt like they were about to pop off her breasts because they were so hard. "Aw shit! Unnnnh!" She came again.

Javier felt her gripping him like a fist. He cocked his back and plunged forward stroking her over and over. Kelis' box was tight. She was wet, and the scent of her sexing body began to appeal to him. "Gimme this pussy! Gimme this pussy! Gimme this pussy! Arrgh!" he growled pounding her out.

Kelis dug her nails into his shoulder blades and screamed again. Javier felt like he was digging into her stomach. He looked into her face and saw her eyes roll back again and again. There was a slight trace of drool in the corner of her mouth that drove him crazy. She was so thick. He knew his cousin wasn't fucking Kelis right. He could tell Peto couldn't handle all the body Kelis had. He slammed forward as hard as he could and felt himself cumming. He pulled out and nutted all over her pussy lips in white ropes. Her cat was shaved clean. The dark brown lips were wide open. Her pink visible to his gaze. He stroked his piece and came hard.

Kelis laid with her thighs wide open. She was out of breath. She couldn't believe what she had just done, but it had been done. She looked down and saw that her middle was coated with Javier's cum and shuddered.

Javier walked over to her on his knees holding his piece. "Here, Baby, you owe me this." He touched her lips with his dick head. His left hand went into her bra and squeezed her hard, left nipple.

She moaned, and grabbed ahold of his dick, before sucking him into her mouth and going to work. She slurped loudly for a full two minutes and popped him out. "Please don't tell, Peto. Please, I will never do this again." She sucked him back into her mouth.

Javier groaned as she took him as far as his sack, pulled him out only to suck him back to the sack again. "Fuck, Peto, I am a boss. He will forever be a worker." He slipped two fingers back into her soiled gap and worked them at full speed.

Kelis sucked him faster and faster. She hated herself but wanted Javier to finish so he could leave. She needed to pray. She needed to wash their sin off her and pray for forgiveness.

Javier pulled out of her mouth and stood up with his piece wet with her saliva. He took a handful of her hair and wiped his pipe off with it. "Time is money, Mami. Call me if you need anything. I wanna fuck that pussy every chance I get." He laughed.

Kelis scooted back against the wall with her knees to her chest. She had five hundred dollars in cash stuck to her ass. "We can never do this again, Javier. Never! I will never cheat on him again."

Javier closed the door to her apartment in her face. "Pay them bills, Mami. Later." He laughed all the way to his Bentley truck, jumped in it and smashed off. Unbeknownst to Peto standing in the gangway across the street from he and Kelis' apartment. He'd witnessed the encounter and was dead set on making his cousin pay for his double-crossing.

Hood Rich

Chapter 2

La Perla, Puerto Rico

Joaquin stepped on the gas to his black nineteen-eighty-four Chevy Caprice Classic. His usual handsome face was a mask of fury. He frowned and tightened his grip on the steering wheel. He pulled down his sun visor as the rays of the sun reflected off the hood of his car and caused him to become momentarily blinded. Light sweat slid down the sides of his face. The air conditioner to his car was broken, and the island of Puerto Rico was experiencing a heatwave like never before. It was so humid that it made it hard for people to breathe, including Joaquin. He looked over to his passenger's seat. Emilia sat with an angry scowl on her beautiful face as well.

"Damn, Mami, you seem like you're more pissed off than me."

"I don't like snitches Joaquin, you know that. We grew up with Pedro; we were all cut from the same cloth. He's making the hood look bad, and for that reason, he has to pay." She adjusted the Mach .11 on her lap.

She had on one black leather glove, and her other hand was freshly manicured. Emilia was a savage in the streets. Her demeanor at times was very tomboyish, but Joaquin knew that underneath it all Emilia was as feminine as they came.

Joaquin increased his speed as he sped through the island. "I feel the same way you feel. Pedro was my homeboy. He tends to have lost his way after going over to America. I still can't believe he brought down so many in Miami from La Perla, it breaks my heart."

"Not mine, I never trusted him. The only reason I never got on his ass is because of you." She pulled her nose. "That's okay though because now I get to do to him what I wanted to do a long time ago." She nodded her head and placed a curly tuft of hair behind her ear. Emilia was a dark-skinned Puerto Rican, with light brown eyes, long curly black hair, and a slim body with a plump derrière that drove most men crazy.

"What makes you think we're about to do anything to him? He is one of us when it's all said and done." Joaquin glanced at her from the side of his eyes, as he turned a corner with the wheels of the tires making a noise. He stepped on the gas again.

Joaquin was five-feet-eight inches tall. He had low hair, with natural curls. His skin complexion was golden. He was Puerto Rican and Black, born and raised in the trenches of La Perla.

"Joaquin, I've known you ever since our mothers used to give us baths in the same sink when we were toddlers. You hate rats. There is nothing you hate more than that." She grabbed ahold of the Mach .11 as they came across a group of islanders that were known for jacking people, cutting their bodies up and throwing them into the Atlantic Ocean. Emilia was ready to shoot at the sight of any movement by them that looked skeptical.

Joaquin had a Tech .9 on his lap, and as he rolled past the Jackers he mugged them and kept driving. They glared at his car. They knew who he was, and he knew what they were all about. So did Emilia, and neither side liked the other. When his car was out of their vicinity Joaquin breathed a sigh of relief. "People who hit women, or abuse children."

"Huh?" Emilia was scanning the streets for any potential threats to them, but now Joaquin had her undivided attention.

"Those are what I hate more than rats or at least just as much as them." He looked over at her.

She nodded. "Yeah, well, you did always say that. Either way, I'm expecting you to make Pedro pay. He earned it, and he has our hood tatted on him which means we are responsible for what he went out there and did. I ain't about to take that shit lightly. So, I'm asking you, Joaquin. Please, let me run point on this one. I'll owe you big time."

Joaquin laughed. "A'ight, I'ma let you do you, but only because you seem to want to handle Pedro so badly. I guess the history between you two is catching up with him."

Emilia cringed. "Throwing a low blow, are we? Perhaps you would like me to hit you with a few low blows regarding Cecilia?" Cecilia was Emilia's older sister by one year and Joaquin's first love.

At the mention of Cecilia's name, Joaquin tensed his muscles and smiled. "A'ight, you got me there. Like I said we're going to let you handle your business. But remember there is a code of silence in La Perla. We don't do that ratting shit. Although we will be fair and hear him out, the paperwork has already vouched for his transgressions. Therefore, he'll just be dealt with by our customs of the island."

Emilia began to shake. "You never needed to say less words than you did with this thing here. I know what I gotta do. Now watch me perform in front of the rest of the crew. I got this shit."

"We gon' see." Joaquin pulled into the wooden garage and cut his engine. "It's showtime."

***

Pedro was shaking like it was twenty below zero outside. His knees knocked together, and his teeth chattered and were clicking together so much that they hurt. It was three o'clock in the afternoon and he found himself placed in a circle inside of a funky, water run downed warehouse where twenty ski-masked bandits stood around him.

The unmasked Joaquin stepped forward with a machete in his hand. He kneeled before Pedro. "You know our customs here in La Perla, Pedro. We are proud, stand up people who keep their mouths shut, and we fight hard to press forward every single day. Our land is our badge of honor. We live for it, and we will die for it. You come from this land. You represent us wherever you are whether we are there or not." Joaquin held the machete out toward him. "What did you do in America? You got one chance to tell me the truth."

Pedro felt like he was about to throw up. He was a big, heavy-set Puerto Rican, with small eyes, and a bald head. "Joaquin, listen to me brother. They had me jammed up. I didn't have a choice. The men I was under were all corrupt. When the Feds came, they had pictures. They knew everything. I did what I had to in order to make it back to the island in one piece."

"What did you do?" Now Joaquin rested the blade of the machete against Pedro's forehead. It was so sharp that the metal began to slide into Pedro's skin. A trickle of blood ran out of him.

Pedro closed his eyes as the blood leaked onto his left lid. "I only told them what I needed to in order to get the proper deal to get back to La Perla. I was there for the hurricane. My mother and Maria with our newborn was here. Joaquin, I had to do what I had to. Please, you would have done the same thing."

Joaquin had been pacing back and forth. He froze when Pedro said this last part. He stepped back in front of him and kneeled down with the machete haphazardly in between his legs. "You think that I would've turned bitch like you and ran my mouth, huh?"

"Joaquin, I wasn't saying it like that. I was saying that you would do anything for your family. You are a true Puerto

18

Rican? You love your mother to tears and Justina as well."
Justina was Joaquin's little sister.

"Even so, I would never ever think to be a rat. I bleed La
Perla. I am the heart of the slums here. My name represents
this island wherever I am. I am a Peralta. I would never dis-
grace this island's representation like you have. Grab him."
Joaquin stood up.

Pedro was grabbed from every angle by cold-hearted savages. They picked him up and slammed him against the wall.
"Joaquin, what's going on? Please don't let them hurt me. I
am your brother. We were potty trained together."

Joaquin closed his eyes. "I could never hurt you, Pedro. I
love Rosalia too much." Rosalia was Pedro's mother.

Emilia slipped in front of Pedro and pulled off her mask.
"But I can, open his mouth."

A big behemoth of a man grabbed Pedro by the throat. As
soon as Pedro opened his mouth two other killas stepped up
and held it open. They pulled both upward and downward
cracking his jaw. The pain was enough to make Pedro scream
at the top of his lungs.

Emilia took the pliers and clamped them down on Pedro's
tongue. She pinched the clampers and began to pull as hard as
she could. "This is what you get for disgracing the island,
Pedro!" She frowned and yanked harder.

Pedro felt like his face was being pulled out of his mouth.
He was in so much pain that all he could do was scream his
head off. His tongue broke away from the tensions that were
on the bottom of his mouth. Blood spurt against his cheek.
Emilia pulled and twisted his tongue until it began to tear
away from the muscles and tissues that kept it locked in place.
Blood dripped over his lip. He fainted just as Emilia gave him
one hard yank and pulled his tongue from his mouth. She

walked it over and dropped it into a Ziploc bag that Joaquin held open for her.

"We will send this back to our brothers in New York that were forced to flee from Miami because of Pedro." Joaquin knelt beside Pedro and smacked him awake. "You are disgraced. While you are in La Perla you will be under arrest until I say you are free. You will be allowed visitors, but that is it. Do I make myself clear?"

Pedro nodded with blood running onto his chest. He cried tears of excruciating pain. He closed his eyes and wondered how he would ever be able to talk again. He thought about his daughter and Maria. He wondered if he would ever be able to have a life with them again?

Emilia stood over him. "If it were up to me, I would take your life for your transgression. Be thankful to be alive, even though you don't deserve it."

Pedro looked up to Emilia with pure hatred. He would find a way to get her back. There was no way he would allow this to be the end result with no form of revenge against what he deemed as his bitter ex. He curled into a ball as he became too dizzy to even think.

"Get him up, and to the hospital before he bleeds out. I don't want to have to explain his death to Rosalia." Joaquin placed his arm around Emilia's neck and headed out of the warehouse and into the scorching La Perla sun.

***

That hot and humid night Joaquin pulled up to the front of Emilia's shack and handed her the bag of cheeseburgers they'd picked up from a restaurant. She took it and sat back in her passenger's seat looking at the shack where she lived as if it were the plague. She took a deep breath, and slowly blew it out.

Joaquin looked up at her colorful shack and back down to her. "What's the matter, Mami? You ain't ready to go in there?"

"I never am, but what can I do. It's all we have left after Hurricane Maria. I'm just tired of being destitute, Joaquin. When is it our time? When will La Perla become great? When will we be able to live a sensible yet comfortable life?"

"Soon, I know it feels right now we are the toilet of the world, but one day soon we are going to be where we need to be. La Perla will be the epicenter of it all and not just someplace where random tourists come to add to our decaying existence." He shook his head. "However, you should know before you walk into that shack Emilia that I love you, and you are my right hand. When I take off there is none other that will be beside me other than you. You're my heart."

Emilia looked at him for a moment and smiled. "Yeah, we'll see." She opened the door to the car. "I'll have Cecilia come down. You stay safe out here tonight. The killers are lurking." She walked away from the car.

Joaquin beeped the horn. "Mamamita, I told you I love you and that's your response to me?"

Emilia shrugged her shoulders. "You know all that sappy shit ain't my thing, Joaquin. But it's all here, though." She beat her fist on her chest.

Joaquin laughed. "Yeah, alright. Well, I still love you girl."

She rolled her eyes and kept walking. "Save it for, Cecilia."

Cecilia came out of the shack with her long hair in a ponytail. "Save what for me?"

"Nothing." Emilia kept walking into the shack and closed the door behind her.

Cecelia stepped up to the passenger's window and bent over. She stuck her head inside the window. "What are you supposed to be saving for me?"

"Nothing, don't worry about, just get in so we can ride. I got some stuff I need to holla at you about."

She opened the door and sat down. As he was pulling away, she closed it and fastened her seat belt. "What's up?"

Joaquin dug between his legs and handed her two thousand dollars. "Here, I need you to use this to pay the bills of your home."

"Joaquin, what are you doing? I told you we would figure it out this month. I can't take this." She held it over his lap.

Joaquin pushed her hand away. "Don't insult me. I know it's hard on your family. I told you that I had you. Don't allow your pride to override your intelligence. Take it, Baby."

Cecilia held the money. "Thank you." She leaned over and kissed his cheek. "I'm going to make sure I perform real well for this tonight. You can bet your bottom dollar on that. She ran her tongue over her lips and moaned seductively.

Joaquin looked over at her. "How is Emilia really doing? I'm worried about her."

Cecilia shrugged her shoulders. "Who really knows? Emilia is Emilia. She only lets people know what she wants them too. Why, what do you think is going on with her?"

"I don't know. Hurricane Maria took your mother's life. I know the two of them were very close. Emilia seems as if she hasn't been the same ever since. Just keep an eye on her for me. That's all I'm getting at."

"You need to be focused more on me, and less on her. How about trying that out for size?" She leaned across the armrest and kissed his soft lips. "You do that, and I'll take care of you. You can be certain of that."

"Oh, is that right?"

"Yeah, that's right."

"Well, we're about to see about that. Why don't you go ahead and get shit started off the right way?" He unzipped his pants.

Cecilia licked her juicy lips and tucked the money into her purse. "I got you, Papi, just fall back and let me twerk this for you."

Hood Rich

Chapter 3

Javier slipped the blue doctor's mask across his face and stuck his hands into a pair of blue latex gloves before he opened the door to the basement of the Asian Cleaners that he and his father Rodolfo were using as a front so they could cook up large quantities of coke before it was distributed all up and down the East coast. As soon as he stepped into the door of the basement, he was hit by a thick cloud of gray Crack smoke. He held his breath and fanned the addictive cloud away from him. He inched further into the trap. The huge basement was filled with workers that were in full effect. There were ten long tables downstairs.

In the middle of each table were two digital scales where the workers weighed up their product before it was placed into an aluminum package and set inside a trunk that already had a tracking device and a cryptic destination location on it. There were six people to each table, three on each side. On one side of the table, there were workers that chopped through the bricks of raw, while on the other side the workers were in charge of weighing the product before wrapping and placing it into the trunk.

There were five armed guards that were responsible for watching the workers every move. They were given directives by both Rodolfo and Javier to kill on sight if they felt that anybody was skimming, or out of line. Things were to run smoothly. Rodolfo didn't tolerate disruptions or theft by any means, both acts were punishable by death.

Javier walked around for a minute until he was sure everything was running as it could be. When he finished his tour, he stepped out of the basement and sniffed the air with his mask off to see if he could smell the strong aroma of the Dope smoke. He could, this worried him. He went to the front of the

Cleaners and waited for Mr. Lee to come out of the back. He could barely smell the atom from where he stood but even a slight stench was enough to cause concern, he didn't want to risk it.

Mr. Lee was a portly, bald Asian man with a round face, and small stature. When he came to the front of the store and saw Javier, he became nervous. The only time he was used to seeing Javier's face was when something was wrong. He plastered a fake smile across his mug. "Javier, what brings you by? How is family?" Mr. Lee's English was broken at best.

"I can smell that shit up here, Lee. You're supposed to make sure I can't smell shit. Now fix that fucking scent or I'm going to have you and all the other Chinese mafuckas down there tied up and on a boat back to China. Do I make myself clear?"

"But we're all Korean, and we don't want no trouble. I fix the scent for you. You smell no more. I make sure for you. Okay?"

"You got two hours." Javier mugged the Asian man with hatred.

Mr. Lee bowed his head. "You need worry no more. I get on it, right way."

***

Javier honked the horn for the third time and grew impatient. It seemed like every time he and Fancy were set to go out, she took her time getting ready. Javier's patience was thinner than an anorexic female. He rolled down the passenger's window as he saw her coming down the driveway of her two-story, white, brick home. It was ninety degrees outside in the middle of March, and the humidity was terrible.

Javier leaned over on the passenger's bucket seats. "Oh, yeah, Mami, you keep taking yo' fuckin' time and I'ma leave yo' punk ass. Time is money. Did you forget that, huh?" He was already drunk off a pint of José Cuervo, and a half bottle of Ace of Spades. He had two Mollies in his system, and sixty milligrams of Percocet, he was lifted.

Fancy hurried to the car on her pigeon toes. "Baby, I'm just trying to look good for you. Damn, what's the rush? You already know you're going to be VIP anyway." She rolled her eyes.

Before she could make it all the way to the car, the door flipped up on the cherry red Hellcat. Javier hopped out with a million dollars' worth of gold jewelry and diamonds around his neck. In the darkness, all the jewelry looked as if it was in 3D. He came around the car with the intention of choking Fancy out. He didn't like no female making him late or standing in the way of his plans. He didn't care if she was his seven-year-old daughter, Vatican's mother.

Fancy dropped and sunk into the Hellcat's seat. "Javier don't start. Let's just have a nice night."

Javier reached into the car and pulled her out. He slung her against the car and wrapped both of his hands around her throat. He choked her as hard as he could. "I'm tired of yo' ass always doing something. You get on my muthafuckin' nerves. This is why I didn't wanna come and get yo' punk ass." He squeezed and squeezed before he eventually let her go.

Fancy fell to the ground, and her short Balenciaga skirt flipped up to her hips. She was without any panties. Her naked vagina was out for all to see. Luckily the only one present was Javier, her daughter's father. "I'm sorry, Javier. Damn, you ain't always gotta go so hard on me!" she hollered, getting up.

27

Javier had visions of rushing her and snatching her up again. He fought the urge. "It's a million-plus bad bitches in Miami. But I'm standing in front of you in all of this drip. I got yo' punk ass rocking Balenciaga's and dripping like a wet mop and you can't have yo' monkey ass ready when I get here. Fuck is wrong with you?" He wiped his mouth. The streetlight reflected off his Patek watch. The face was flooded in yellow diamonds that offset his Chanel fit, and Balenciaga shoes.

Fancy pulled her skirt down. She could still feel his hands around her neck. She swallowed and it hurt. "I'm sorry, Javier, but you don't always have to go so hard on me. You make it seem like you hate me or something." Fancy was caramel-skinned, with brown eyes, and a slim frame. She had a rounded backside, and small B cup breasts that she felt were just perfect.

"Bitch, if I hated you I wouldn't fuck wit' you at all. But my time is precious, and if I dare to spend it with you, you're supposed to make that shit worth my while. I'm a mutha-fuckin' boss. You are a kept bitch, meaning I make sure that everything you need is provided for. The least you can do is have yo' ass on time. You don't know what the fuck I got go-ing on tonight." He walked around and sat in the driver's seat closing the doors.

Fancy crossed her arms in front of her. "I'm sorry, next time I will make sure I am prepared ahead of time. But in my defense, the majority of the times you tell me we are going out, you never show up. So, I really don't know what to do or if you're coming or not."

Javier knew she was right, but his pigheadedness wouldn't allow him to agree with her openly. He felt like he needed to keep his foot on her neck, and that's the route he chose to travel. "Bitch, then you just give me the benefit of the doubt because life doesn't revolve around you. You got that shit?"

28

"Yeah, I got it," she replied, looking dejected. She made her way to the passenger side of the car and got in.

Javier looked over to her. "How is my daughter doing?" He cruised to a stop at the end of the block before stepping on the gas again. The blue ground effects under the Hellcat made the streets light up as he drove down them.

"She misses you like crazy. You're all she talks about. You really should try to work spending some time with her into your schedule. It could do both of you some good."

"Oh, so now you're telling me how to be a father? Fuck you think gives you that right when you dropped out of school at sixteen, and you ain't been on shit since then?"

"Damn, Javier, you always gotta make shit so personal. I wasn't saying it to take a shot at you. I was just trying to tell you how much your daughter loves and adores you, that's it. Please forgive me for putting my two cents in whatever you two have going on."

"Right, this shit gets hot quick when you get to spitting that bullshit don't it?" He laughed and popped another Percocet. His body already felt heavy, his eyelids were low.

"And besides, I guess the nail salon and the restaurant means that I haven't been on nothing, huh?"

"Who opened those businesses for you, and whose name is at the top of all of the paperwork?" Javier popped his collar. "Bitch, I'm in control, and it's like I said you ain't been on shit."

Fancy felt small, she hated Javier at times. While he helped her in certain areas where she needed support, he often made her feel belittled and as if her efforts to make it ahead in life were futile. "Well, anyway, Vatican loves you, and I hope you see her soon." She rested her chin on her hand and looked out the window.

***

Javier sat in the VIP section at Black Diamonds, a famous location for A-list celebrities and music icons. Black Diamonds were also where the upper echelon of the dope game went to mingle and flaunt their status. Javier made sure that his million-dollars' worth of jewelry was being hit just right by the light. He slid on his Dolce and Gabbana gold frames and sat back with two gold bottles of Moët, sipping from one at a time. The club was packed, and from his location, he was able to see the majority of the people that were there.

Fancy sat beside him in a depressed mood. All the things that Javier had said to her were beginning to eat away at her womanhood. She felt less than human. She did need to get up and out on her own. For a woman to sit back and allow a man to do everything for them was completely lazy, and idiotic. It was March of twenty-twenty in the year of the woman. Most of the females in Miami were out getting it on their own. She needed to be one of them.

Sudan was a dark-skinned, thick, gorgeous, almond-eyed Africa woman from the place that she was named after in Africa. She stepped up to Javier's velvet ropes with two Sudanese women equally as fine as her standing behind her. All three had tribal accented make up on their faces that allowed them to stand out. Sudan took her index finger and motioned for Javier to meet her at the ropes.

Javier pointed to himself. When Sudan nodded, he got up and made his way to the ropes. His neck felt like it was being weighed down by all the jewelry. He pulled his left sleeve back to showcase his iced Patek. His eyes zoomed into Sudan's. "What's good, Mami? I see you jockin' me from afar."

"You and I need to have a sit down to discuss some business. Word on the strip is that you are the man from La Perla."

Javier looked around, he frowned at her. "If you were given the right word then they woulda told you that you don't get to talk directly to me without an invitation. Go get your shit in order, then come and fuck with me." He turned around to walk away.

"Africa is interested in doing business with you. I am an ambassador to Sudan sent by our Royals to personally do business with Mr. Rodolfo and his prince. I take that to be you and not Joaquin." She lowered her eyes.

'How the hell did she know about my little brother Joaquin and my father's name?' Javier thought. He stepped closer to the ropes. "Who did you say was again?"

"My name is, Sudan, like the nation I represent. We are very interested in merging with the Peralta's. We are looking to invest some fine gems along with a lot of money that will make you and your people very happy. All I need is a few hours of your time." She ran her tongue across her succulent green painted lips and smiled, never taking her eyes away from his.

Javier snapped his fingers. "Let them through, Sudan you come over here and you sit by me."

Hood Rich

Chapter 4

It was three weeks after Pedro had returned to the island to seek refuge from the many killers looking to track him down back in America, only to be caught by Joaquin and his crew of La Perla savages and had his tongue ripped out of his mouth at Joaquin's behest. Joaquin was back home after navigating the treacherous slums of Puerto Rico for two days straight looking for a way to make ends meet. He tiptoed down the short hallway, and into the kitchen until he was standing right behind Martina.

He smirked, then he slid his arm around her neck. "Hey, beautiful."

She jumped and elbowed him in the ribs, then she grabbed a steak knife out of the dish wringer and held it to his throat before she noticed that it was her son. At the acknowledgment of him, she eased back and took a deep breath with the steak knife in her hand.

She slowly exhaled. "What are you crazy?"

The right side of Joaquin's ribs pounded as if he'd been hit by a car. He was in pain. "You're asking me if I'm crazy, really? Mama you just nearly killed me and all I was trying to do was to steal a kiss from you." He rubbed his ribs. "Good Lord have mercy."

"I never taught you to steal. You want anything in life you ask for it, or you work hard for it. With me, your mama, you ask." She pointed at her cheek. "Kiss me, son, I miss it so much." She closed her eyes.

Joaquin pressed his lips to her cheek and kissed her. Then he grabbed her to him and turned her around so he could look into her eyes. "I missed you the last few days. How have you been?"

"I'm alive, that's more than I can say for a bunch of our people that lost their lives in Hurricane Maria." She shook her head. "I still can't believe that they named the storm after my mother. What a life." She tried to get out of his embrace, but he held her. "Son, let me go."

"Mama, how are you really?" He kissed her forehead.

She popped his shoulder. "So much affection from you. Even when you were just a boy. You've always loved your mother. You're something else." She tried to get out of his embrace again.

He picked her up and twirled her around in the air. She yelped, and he laughed. "You're my mother. I love you more than anybody in existence." He held her in the air and planted kisses all over her face.

"Let me down, Joaquin. Do it!" She slapped him.

He ducked her blows and kissed her whenever she moved her hands in a certain way so he could get to her face. "I love you, Ms. Meanie, and I can kiss you whenever I want to." He kissed her five more times before placing her back on her feet.

She stood before him in her four-foot-eleven-inch glory blushing. "You are a man that I do not know who you take after. There is none like my son." She walked up to him and placed her hands on his shoulders. "Never change your soul baby. You give me hope that one day men will be like you again. You are my strength. I hope you know that." She stared at him for a moment, then she kissed his right cheek.

Whenever Martina kissed Joaquin, he felt like he was given the strength to accomplish anything in life. He cleared her hair from her face and smiled down at his Queen. "I will always be me, mama. You know that."

Justina opened her bedroom door and rolled her eyes at them. "Yeah, you'll always be a butt face." She snickered and eased into the kitchen wearing a pair of daisy dukes that were all up in her butt. Her tank top was cut halfway off. She was without a bra.

She grabbed two Soda Pops out of the refrigerator and was on her way back to her room with her cheeks jiggling out of her shorts. She was about to close the door when Joaquin put two and two together. He sped in front of her and walked into her room before she could. He noticed the window to her bedroom was wide open, but the expanse of the room appeared to be empty.

"Get out of my room, Joaquin, dang." Justina cried following behind him with both of her hands full.

"Who is in here?" he whispered low enough so that their mother wouldn't hear him.

"Joaquin, please just go. Don't nobody be all up in your business when you do whatever it is that you be doing," she whispered.

"Tell me who's here because if I find them myself, I'm putting them out. Then you and I are going to have a major problem." He walked to her closet and placed his hand on the doorknob.

"Wait." Justina closed the door to her bedroom all the way. She bumped Joaquin out of the way. "We were just about to have a little fun when mama went to sleep." She pulled open the closet door and a younger female her age, along with a male was hiding behind the few clothes that she possessed.

The female had on a small pair of cotton shorts, and a tank top, while the male had on shorts and was shirtless. They came out of the closet and stood behind Justina. The female kissed Justina's neck and held her around the waist possessively.

Martina knocked on the door. "What's going on in there?"

Justina held her hands in prayer fashion. "Please, please, please don't get me in trouble, Joaquin."

Joaquin shook his head. "Y'all better be using protection."

Justina bent over the bed and slid her hand under the pillows on her bed. She came up with two condoms. She looked over her shoulder at him. Her shorts disappeared completely in her middle. "We are."

Joaquin caught the boy checking out Justina's ass and the barely covered gap between her legs, he wanted to snap, especially because she was without underwear, so her full sex was displayed for his eyes. Instead of raining on her parade he eased out of the room and placed his arm around Martina's neck. "Come on, mama, let's talk bills. Where are we?"

Martina spun from under his neck. "No, no, no, that's the last thing that I want to talk about. I'm tired, I've been up all day, and I've already taken my sleep medication. I love you, son, but I will see you in the morning." She held his face while she kissed his cheek. She walked away from him and disappeared into her room, then she closed her door and locked it.

Joaquin was having second thoughts on letting Justina do whatever she had planned under his mother's roof. He stepped to her door ready to knock on it and kick out her company when he heard Justina moan loudly. Her bed began to squeak, then there was a pounding at the front door. He stood perplexed before he turned on the balls of his feet and went to answer the door. When he got there, he found Emilia standing there with tears running down her face. He was ready to run into the house to grab his .9 millimeter.

She struggled to catch her breath. "Justice died, he got hit by a car. I want you to help me bury him." She turned her back and walked off.

***

Emilia stood in the back of the cemetery in La Perla, threw the last bit of dirt on her Pitbull and slammed the shovel into the dirt. She wiped a lone tear that sailed down her face and sniffled. "Justice was the last piece of my mother that I had left now she's gone entirely." She fell to her knees and bawled her eyes out.

Joaquin kneeled beside her and slid his arm around her shoulder. She got up right away and walked a short distance away from him. He stood up and dusted off his hands. "Emilia, you're not alone in this. I got your back. I hope you know that?"

Emilia nodded and looked up at the stars. It was a dark night and the stars were extra bright and shining. They could see the Milky Way as clear as day. "Sometimes I wish I was an astronaut."

Joaquin stepped beside her. "Why, what's so good about being one of those?"

"Because then I could get far far away from the island. There is nothing in La Perla but heartache and pain. The breeze coming off the ocean makes me cringe now. I hate it here." She frowned and mugged the sky.

"La Perla is home, San Juan is our birthplace. It is our land to protect. It brings us great comfort."

"La Perla is a place of pain and agony. Our island is in destruction. Nobody cares about us, not even the mayor. She is too busy kissing the American president's ass to care about her own people. Here we are suffering, and she is somewhere in Miami living in a mansion while we struggle to find clean water. La Perla is hell and you know it," she said this in his face and walked off.

Joaquin stood with his head down. He felt both angered and defeated. He looked up at the sky and exhaled loudly. "Emilia, if we don't have La Perla then what do we have?"

Emilia took a seat in the dirt that overlooked the long road of sixty-fifth that ran through the city of La Perla. "All we have is distant memories of what our island used to be. There used to be happiness here. There used to be unity, and family. Now it is infested with drugs and famine. Diseases are natural here. Starving families is a regular sight. We kill each other as if we are outsiders, and not all Puerto Ricans from the same land. My heart is turning colder daily, Joaquin. I don't know how much more of this island I can take."

There was a rustle in the graveyard, Joaquin turned to see where the noise came from. In walked four jackers. They were wearing leather jackets with ski masks on their faces. Despite their masks, both Joaquin and Emilia knew who they were. Joaquin searched his waist for his gun and cursed under his breath. He'd left it in the car. The Jackers came and surrounded the pair.

Emilia stood up and held out her arms. "What the fuck do y'all want? We don't have any money on us, just beat it."

One of the Jackers stepped in Joaquin's face and sized him up. "What's up, Joaquin?"

Joaquin didn't know who he was exactly but at the mention of his name, he knew it was beef. He balled up his fists. "We're burying a loved one. How about you mafuckas leave so we can finish this ceremony." He felt himself getting heated.

The head Jacker shook his head as two more members of his crew stepped into the graveyard. "This here is Jack Boy turf. It seems like y'all burying whatever it is you are burying in unsanctioned dirt. Who gave you permission?"

Emilia didn't want to waste time with the formalities. This was Puerto Rico, when it was on it was on. She bawled her fists as tight as she could, ran up to the lead Jacker and punched him hard as she could, dropping him to the dirt where he was knocked out cold. She jumped up and stomped him in the stomach knocking the wind out of him.

"Fuck you, muthafuckas!" she hollered and took off swinging on the masked man closest to her. She dropped him as well. Then she was punched in the jaw hard. She staggered back dizzy.

Joaquin punched her attacker and picked him up slamming him with all his strength breaking his back. A rib poked through his side. Joaquin stomped him three times before he was tackled to the ground. Emilia kneed the man off him. She fell on top of the man swinging with blow after blow connecting each time, busting his nose, then his eye. She was kicked in the back and flew past Joaquin.

Joaquin jumped up swinging and connecting over and over. He grew tired, then three men jumped on him at once. He was overpowered, they beat him into the dirt, stomping, and kicking. Two men jumped on Emilia doing the same. Both friends were beaten severely and left for dead. After the police pulled up to the graveyard five minutes later the Jackers took off running. Joaquin crawled over to Emilia who was knocked out. He had blood coming out of his nose and mouth, he also had two broken ribs that pained him. He hugged up to her and kissed her cheek before he passed out from blood loss.

Hood Rich

Chapter 5

It was late Friday afternoon the sun was brightly shining on a warm and clear day. Javier held the back door open for his daughter Vatican and allowed her to climb into his brand- new black on black Range Rover that he'd driven off the lot that morning. This was only his third time picking her up from her school since she'd started going to the Private School.

"How is my baby doing?" He closed the door behind her and rushed around to the driver's seat.

"I'm doing fine, Daddy. I can't believe you're picking me up from school. Mama didn't tell me anything," she said this to him in Spanish. She tried to make it a habit whenever she spoke to Javier that she did so in Spanish because that's what he'd told her to do. He wanted her to stay as close to her Spanish roots as possible.

"Well, I didn't tell you because he told me not to." Fancy looked over her shoulder to make sure Vatican was clicked into her seat belts, once she confirmed that she was she turned back around to stare out of her passenger's window.

Javier smiled while looking into the rearview mirror of his truck. "I wanted to surprise you, Princess. What you ain't happy to see your daddy or something?" Javier pulled away from the school and turned up the air-conditioning.

"Yes, Daddy I am. I still can't believe you're here, though. What are we going to do today?"

"Anything you want to do, Princess. I was thinking that we stop by the fair today so daddy can win you some stuffed animals and all that good stuff. But before or after the fair we can do whatever you wanna do because it is your day. How does that sound?"

"Great DaddySong, oh my God I'm so happy. Mama isn't he the greatest daddy ever created in the whole wide world?" Vatican was excited out of her mind.

Fancy raised both of her eyebrows. Not only did she silently disagree but she honestly felt that Javier ranked amongst the top with some of the worst dads. Though he provided for them to an extent he always made sure that Fancy knew what he was doing, and that she also knew that if it wasn't for him she wouldn't have anything. He was very egotistical. Instead of Fancy saying anything she chose to hold her silence.

This angered Javier. "Fancy, you ain't hear what my little girl just asked you?" He was as calm as he possibly could be, but Fancy was already getting on his nerves and he didn't like it.

"No, I'm sorry baby, my mind was somewhere else. What were you saying?" She played it off as best as she could. She just didn't think she had it in her to agree to such foolishness. She knew the truth about Javier, and he was trifling.

"I said isn't my daddy the greatest daddy ever?" Vatican was giddy.

"Sure, baby, if that's how you feel that's awesome." 'Forget all about mommy, who does all she can to make it happen for you every single day even when your fuckin' father ain't nowhere to be found, it's cool,' Fancy thought.

Javier glared at her from the side of his eyes. He nodded his head. He could tell how Fancy really felt and it irritated him to his very core. "Baby, just sit back and relax, we're about to cruise for a second. Do you wanna go to the fair first, or do you wanna go shopping first?"

"Can I get some new electronics when we go shopping with my clothes?" Vatican wanted to see exactly what Javier had in mind and what she could get away with.

"Sure, baby, like I said it's your day. So, whatever you want it's all about you," Javier reiterated.

"Then daddy let's go shopping first. We can always go to the fair later because I need a new iPad and some video games for my Xbox. Wow, this day is so amazing already."

"A'ight babysit back and put on your headphones. I need to talk some grown-up stuff with mommy for a second." Javier glanced into the rearview mirror to make sure she was following his commands. When he saw that she was he waited for a second before he called her name over and over. Once he was sure she couldn't hear him he turned to Fancy. "Bitch what do you want me to do different, huh? I am trying the best I can. This shit ain't easy for me."

Fancy felt like she was being accosted by a crazy person. "What the hell are you talking about now, Javier?"

"Ain't no now it's period, bitch. You don't think I can tell what you really wanted to say when my daughter was giving me props about being the best daddy in the world? I could see that you wanted to shoot that shit down, but you held your tongue and it was probably in your best interest."

"Damn, I don't feel like going through this with you today. I swear I just wanted to have a nice family day without all the drama. Can you chill with that shit, please?" Fancy scrunched her face.

"Family day?" Javier scoffed. "Bitch, Vatican, is the only family I got in this truck. You ain't nothing but the womb that housed my little girl until it was time for her to come out. That's it, don't get shit twisted. We ain't family, and we ain't friends. I can do a lot better than you. I mean, look at what the fuck you rolling in." He laughed and popped his Versace collar.

Fancy rolled her eyes. "You're so fuckin' materialistic that it's disgusting. After dealing with you for so many years you make it easy for a girl to be willing to fall in love with a bum type of man just so things can be built from the ground up by both he and I. I don't know how you turned out like this, but ugh."

"Ugh?" He licked his right pinky and thumb then rubbed them over his eyebrows. "Ain't shit ugh about me. You know what I gotta do when I get back to the house, I gotta count a million dollars in cash." He cracked up. "That's a million fuckin' dollars and you think I give a fuck about you saying ugh to me?" He smacked his lips. "This coming from a bitch that's twenty-five just like me but ain't got a pot to piss in outside of me. How do they say that shit in English? Girl, bye." He broke out laughing again and had to swerve the truck because he came close to hitting a smaller car that was in front of them.

Fancy kept her head down. "I'm not always going to be down like this, Javier. I won't always need you. One day you're not going to be able to throw this type of stuff in my face. I'll be able to stand on my own two feet. I'll be independent of you and everybody else, just you watch."

"Yeah, the fuck right. Outside of that little modeling, you did a few years ago, you ain't never been shit, and you ain't never gon' be shit. But like I said before, we ain't family. The only mafucka I care about in this truck outside of myself is Vatican. So, keep that shit in your bum ass mind as much as you can and we'll be alright." He scoffed again. "Oh, and you're lucky she didn't ask me if she had the best mother in the world I woulda gave yo' ass the bidness. Be lucky I'm letting you come wit' us today. Keep yo' mouth shut, and you might get a bag or somethin'. Keep talking and you might get flatlined either way ain't neither one of them gon' hurt me, know that." He reached under his seat and sat a .45 on his lap. "I'm just saying."

Fancy felt so low that at that moment she wanted to make him kill her. She was ready to be rid of him. She no longer cared about the financial aspect of his providing whenever he chose to actually do it. She didn't care how his absence would affect, Vatican. She just wanted him out of their lives, and the sooner the better. She was so angry that she wanted to punch him. But like a submissive woman she held her tongue and her comments to herself even though doing so was slowly killing her.

"That's what the fuck I thought." Javier turned up his Reggaeton music and began nodding his head.

***

Kelis took Alexis out of the sink and dried her off. She rubbed her nose against her one-year-old daughter's. "You're so pretty. You're so beautiful, little Mami." She kissed Alexis's little stomach and made the baby laugh while she kicked her little feet. Kelis finished drying her off and got her dressed for bed. She picked her up, just as the front door to their apartment opened and Peto staggered inside holding himself up against the wall. Kelis rolled her eyes.

Peto wiped his mouth with the back of his hand. "Good afternoon to you, too." He laughed and stood up straight trying to hold his eyes open.

"Alexis needs more diapers, Peto. Did you get some when you went out or did you forget again?" She carried the baby to the nursery and placed her inside the crib. She tucked her in just right and swaddled her.

Peto held his weight up by the use of the door frame. "They were sold out," he lied.

Kelis looked over her shoulder at him. "What?"

"See I went to the gas station to get the pampers but they said somebody had just bought the last pack." He hiccupped. "So, then I walked down to the Walmart thinking I would have better luck there, but it turns out that it was more of the same thing. No one got no Pampers probably until the morning. I'll go and try again then. She should be straight overnight right?" He was slurring his words so bad that she could barely understand him.

"Peto, you know I hate it when you lie to me." She kissed Alexis and backed out of the nursery after turning on the Baby Monitor that her parents had bought for them. Peto made an attempt to go over and kiss Alexis as well until she pulled him away from the crib. "I don't like it when she inhales all that alcohol that is on your clothes. It could affect her later." She pulled him out of the room and closed the door.

Peto stood staring at her. "Why did you say that I lied to you?"

Kelis waved him off. "Not tonight, Peto, I already have a migraine starting to form." She left him standing in the hallway, grabbed the broom from the pantry and began sweeping the kitchen.

Peto came into the kitchen and looked over his wife. "Am I more than a loser to you?"

"I don't think you're a loser, Peto. I just don't think you try hard enough to be a man. You give up too easily. Your standards aren't high enough." She swept the small amount of trash into a pile and picked it up with a dustpan.

"What is my purpose, Kelis? If I am nothing more than a loser. Then what is my fuckin purpose?" He punched his fist into his hand.

Kelis dismissed him as throwing a tantrum. She had very little respect for him. In her book, any man that didn't provide for his family was not to be taken seriously. Sometimes Peto irked her soul. She didn't want to be around him, but then she had to remember that he was her husband and she vowed to love him for better or for worse. "Peto, you need to calm down, and then go and get you some rest. You're drunk, and when you are drunk you only manage to think about the negative things."

"Do you love me, Kelis? I need you to be honest with me, right here, right now."

"Yes, I love you. You are my husband, and I will love you until my last breath."

"Then come over here and kiss my lips. I feel so broken right now, I need you to heal me." He held his arms open.

Kelis dumped the trash into the garbage and replaced the broom and dustpan. "I don't feel like being lovey-dovey tonight. Today has been rough, and I don't know how Alexis is going to make it through the night. Just go to bed." She waved him off and stepped past him.

The scent of her perfume permeated to his nose and reminded him of those simple times when both of them were able to cuddle and just be in love. His stomach turned over, he felt sick.

"Kelis, baby, come and talk to me for a minute. We need to get an understanding about a few things." He heard her close their bedroom door. He stood for a moment stuck wallowing in his own pity before he pulled himself together and left the house again.

Kelis sat in her bed alone for ten minutes with tears streaming down her face before she picked up her phone and sent Javier a text. As soon as she finished the text, she sent it before she lost her nerve to do so. She placed her hands over her face and cried her eyes out. Then she sank to her knees in prayer.

***

"That's three cases back there. Alexis shouldn't need no Pampers for a while but should these run out make sure you call and let me know right away. I told you, I got you, Mami." Javier grabbed the cases of Pampers from the backseat and placed them in front of a solemn Kelis.

"Thank you, Javier. I hate that I had to lean on you again, but soon Alexis will be old enough to attend daycare and I can work some. I really appreciate you, though."

Javier leaned into her face. "Hey, Mami, stop that. You're my little baby, right?"

She lowered her head. "I think so."

"Don't think so, know so. I got all this money, and I don't know what to do with it all. I am supposed to be spending it on a dime like you. So, it's all good. You're my baby, gimme kiss." He pulled five thousand out of his pocket to entice her.

Kelis felt her willpower slipping at the sight of the money that her household so desperately needed. "But, Peto."

Javier pulled her long hair and brought her face to his own. He kissed her lips and slipped his hand underneath her short cotton dress.

"I don't give a damn about, Peto. Peto isn't a man, I am. He needs to grow up." He kissed along her cheek and bit onto her neck while his fingers worked in between her thighs.

Kelis closed her eyes and allowed Javier her savior to take her to an orgasm that had her screaming loudly in the Range Rover. She felt guilty, she felt sinful, but at the same time, she felt what Javier said was the truth. Peto wasn't a man, and that he really needed to grow up.

Javier brought her to two quick orgasms and tucked the money back inside of his pocket with a wicked smile on his face. He pulled his wet fingers out of her. "Remember if you need anything just give me a call." He leaned over her lap and opened the door for her to get out.

Hood Rich

Chapter 6

"Well, you're a sight for sore eyes." Joaquin joked as he walked up on Emilia who was sitting on the hood of a white Lexus in a pair of tight purple Capri pants. He held his ribs as he walked closer. It was only three weeks after both he and Emilia had been jumped in the cemetery by the Jackers, both were still feeling the pains of their injuries.

Emilia stepped away from the car and walked up to him. Her left eye was still a bit black underneath from where she'd sustained a series of punches from the Jackers. "You're still hurting I see?" She was too but she didn't want to show her weaknesses in front of Joaquin.

"My ribs, it's no big deal." The sun was bright, though the sky was a bit cloudy. Every so often a cloud would block the sun to give them a brief version of relief from its scorching rays.

"I did some digging. I found out that the leader of the Jackers' name is Vinny. Vinny isn't even Puerto Rican, he's from the Dominican Republic, and so are a few more of the guys in their crew. Vinny is kind of connected. His brother Rank runs guns for some major people out of San Juan and the Dominican Republic. So, if we have any thoughts of going at them, we have to be ready to die."

Joaquin stepped into her face. "That's how we go at everything. This is La Perla."

Emilia nodded, she had her long curly hair in two pigtails. She smelled like Jasmine. The scent was appealing to Joaquin. "So, what do you wanna do?"

Joaquin rubbed his chin. "Where is their hang out? Is there a certain place we can catch them slipping? If so I wanna know about it."

"Emilia! Emilia!" Franco called from the doorway to Emilia's colorful shack.

"Hold that thought, Joaquin." She jogged away from him.

Joaquin was trying to see if he recognized Franco's face. When he saw that he didn't, his muscles tensed. Especially when Emilia ran up to Franco, placed her arms around his neck and kissed his lips. Joaquin felt like somebody had stabbed him through the heart with a harpoon. His knees got weak, then he got angry.

Emilia grabbed a hold of Franco's hand and brought him to Joaquin. "Joaquin this, Franco. Franco this, Joaquin, my best friend."

Franco was slim with curly hair, and a handsome face. He had a mole on the right side of his thick lips. His arms were ripped and so was his abs. He was without a shirt and smelled like Axe body spray. Franco held out his hand for Joaquin to shake.

Joaquin glared at him. "Who are you?"

Emilia stepped in between both men. She turned her back to Franco and backed him up just a tad. Then she looked up to Joaquin. "Joaquin Franco is my fiancé. He is from New York, and in a few months, I am going there so I can marry him. He is a real estate mogul and is very connected in the music industry."

Joaquin turned his back to them. He placed his hand over her heart. At the simple mention that Emilia was set to be married, he felt like his heart had stopped. Suddenly the pain in his ribs became so immense that he nearly doubled over. He dropped to one knee.

Emilia rushed to his side. "Joaquin, are you okay?"

Joaquin grimaced in pain. He gritted his teeth and forced himself to stand up. He looked Emilia over as if seeing her for the first time, then looked back at Franco. He wanted to murder him. He turned to Emilia. "Marriage, when were you going to tell me this?"

Franco saw what it was, he held up his hand. "Baby, I'll meet you back inside." He turned and left.

Emilia waited until he was inside of her shack before she addressed the comment Joaquin had made. "Look, I told you I wanted out of La Perla. I'm sick of Puerto Rico period. I hate it here now. Every day I am reminded of all the pain that this island beholds. Now Franco is well connected, and he comes from a very rich family. When I used to visit my cousins in the South Bronx during the summer, he and I were summer-time girlfriend and boyfriend. Just so happens that he never forgot about me when he got older. Now he wants me to be his wife, and if it means that I get to leave this life behind then I am all for it."

"I never thought I'd see the day when you turned your back on me. You make me sick, Emilia." He held his taped ribs and walked away from her.

Emilia stood there for a moment watching him. She felt a heavy heart take over her spirit. She had never meant to cross Joaquin. She was only doing what was best for her. She jogged and caught up to him and began walking beside him. The clouds had disappeared, and the sun was shining full force. "Joaquin, what do you want from me? I'm twenty years old and I am unhappy with where I am in life. Franco offers me a healthy alternative. Am I not supposed to take it?"

Joaquin felt like his heart was broken. He didn't know how to tell Emilia how he was feeling without sounding soft, or as if he was overstepping his bounds. It didn't help that he was screwing Cecilia. "Look, you gotta do what's best for you. Don't worry about me. I'll be okay, I just wish you woulda told me this when you started putting all this together. It woulda saved me a lot of time and energy. Go live your best life Emilia. I don't even care anymore."

Emilia winced in emotional pain and abandonment. "You don't mean that." She stopped mid-stride.

"Yes, I do. You're not the only one that can shut off your emotions." He kept walking with his eyes burning. It was at this moment that he revealed to himself that he was nuts over Emilia, and the thought of her marrying Franco, or any man for that matter crushed his soul.

Emilia watched Joaquin walk away until he disappeared. Then she traipsed back to her shack with her mind running rampant with crazy thoughts. She felt like she'd lost more than her best friend. The worst emotional pain she'd ever felt plagued her. She felt lost and confused.

***

Emilia took a deep breath and slowly blew it out. She stepped up to Joaquin's door and knocked with butterflies in her stomach. It was nine o'clock on a rainy night. She was dressed in her best skirt and matching pink top. Her hair was pulled back into a ponytail and she was hoping there was a way for her to salvage the night before the entire day was ruined.

Martina answered the door with a big cake mixing bowl in her hand. She whipped the chocolate cake and smiled over it at Emilia. "Emilia, how are you, my daughter?"

"I'm good, Ms. Peralta. Is Joaquin home?"

Martina moved out of the way and waved Emilia inside. She allowed Emilia to walk in front of her. She checked out her figure and how much she had grown up from the time when she was just a little girl. "Emilia, you are beautiful. You always have a mean scowl on your face. How will any man ever know how pretty you are?" Martina hugged her.

Emilia shrugged her shoulders and felt so uneasy. "May I go back and see if he will talk to me?"

"Sure, Baby, you want to stay for a piece of my famous La Perla chocolate cake? It is made with struggle and love."

"No thank you, Ms. Peralta." She made her way through the small shack until she came upon Joaquin's door. She knocked on it.

Joaquin was sitting on the bed loading up a Mach .11. He'd placed the twenty other bullets inside of it with four to go. He took his time. "Go away, I'm busy right now."

"Joaquin, it's Emilia. I need to speak to you." She felt nervous.

Joaquin froze for a second. Then he stood up and placed the Mach .11 on the dresser. "Uh, give me a second." He wiped the sweat from his face and exhaled slowly. He felt frantic. He walked to the door and opened it. "What do you want?"

Emilia frowned at him. "Boy, I need to talk to you. And is that any kind of way to greet somebody?" She brushed past him. Her arm slid across the skin of his naked chest. 'Damn why did he have to be without a shirt tonight? Lord help me.'

Joaquin closed the door. "So, what is going on now? Are you coming to tell me that you're pregnant now, too, and that maybe you're leaving for New York?"

Emilia rolled her eyes. "No, it's nothin' like that." She turned her back to him and rubbed her sweaty palms together. "Ever since you walked away from me today, I haven't been able to think about anything else other than you. I don't like feeling like I am betraying you or crossing you in any way. You are my best friend and my first loyalties have always been to you, Joaquin."

"Sure, doesn't feel like it? Why didn't you tell me that you were about to marry that pretty boy? Didn't you think that I woulda wanted to know?" He felt sick all over again. He still couldn't believe she was getting married.

"I'm sorry, Joaquin, but I didn't know how to break it down to you. I feel quite guilty honestly. I can't imagine life without you being just down the road. I don't know how I am going to do it." She hung her head and took a seat on the bed.

Joaquin began to shake. He stepped beside Emilia feeling like he was about to fall apart. "Emilia, I will do anything. I don't care what it is."

"What are you talking about?" She asked looking up and finding tears ready to well over in Joaquin's eyes. "Oh, my God."

Joaquin dropped to one knee. He took her hand. "Emilia, I don't understand what is going on with me, but I can't lose you, not now, not ever. I love you with all my heart and soul. I will kill anyone of those Cabròns over you. Franco isn't ready to die for you. I am, I will die for you in a heartbeat. I bleed for you, Emilia." Tears ran down his face from the anger of imagining life without Emilia. He saw a picture of Franco hugging up to Emilia and having sex with her and it was enough to make Joaquin go out and kill him.

Emilia stood up, she was lost. "Joaquin, you are dating Cecilia. Cecelia loves you. You and I can never be together because you are my best friend, and you've already slept with my sister. So, what am I supposed to do? Please tell me!" She grew angry and snatched her hand away from him.

Joaquin grabbed her and pushed her against the wall. He stepped into her face until their foreheads were on each other's. "I don't love nobody but you, Emilia. You are my heart. You are the nourishment to my soul. Please don't marry, Franco, I need you."

"But, Joaquin, I—"

Joaquin kissed her lips and wrapped his arm around her body. He pulled her close to him and increased the intensity of his kiss. "I love you." More kissing, his hands slid down her lower back until he was gripping her ass.

Emilia moaned, and stepped into his kiss. She could smell his sweat, it mixed with his deodorant. The scent heightened her arousal. She closed her eyes and found herself melting into the oasis that was Joaquin. She imagined how things could be if they were together. She moaned louder and sunk into him. But then suddenly Cecelia's face entered her mind. She imagined Cecelia in tears. She broke the kiss and backed away. Her kitty dripping, her nipples were harder than she had ever imagined them being before. She was panting for oxygen.

"Joaquin, we can't. Cecelia loves you. I don't want to hurt my sister or Franco."

Joaquin adjusted his erection. Emilia diverted her eyes so as to not embarrass him. "Emilia, what if I talk to Cecelia and tell her how I feel? What if I tell her that I love you and that I have always been in love with you? Will, you be my—"

"Your what, Joaquin? Your wife? Your girlfriend? Your best friend? What do you want me to be to you? Or are you just jealous of Franco because he wants to take me away from this hellhole? You don't even know what you want me to be to you, do you?" She stepped into his face challenging him.

Joaquin held his silence, he was confused. He had never thought things through thoroughly when it came to their relationship beyond their friendship. "Damn."

"Yeah, damn is right. We don't have no money, no home, no sense of direction. Franco seems to be the only outlet I have from La Perla. I don't wanna be trapped here forever. I love you just as much as you love me, but I have to marry Franco.

He's my only escape, I'm sorry." She kissed his cheek and left his bedroom.

Joaquin fell to his knees and broke down like he had never done before in his life. He tilted his head back and cried out to God in heaven. He begged him for a way to make Emilia his, even if it meant through murder. He prayed so long and hard that he wound up sleeping right there on the floor at the foot of his bed.

Chapter 7

Javier looked across the boardroom's table at his father Rodolfo. Rodolfo was typing away on his laptop finalizing a few last-minute business ventures in the interest of sugar cane coming out of Cuba. When he finished, he closed his laptop and glanced down at his Rolex watch. Rodolfo was a handsome man, with black and gray hair that fit him just fine. For a man of fifty, he was physically fit and muscular, with a salt and pepper goatee.

"She's late." He frowned at Javier.

"She's just landed upstairs. She texted me about two minutes ago. You're so impatient, Papi. Take a load off, it's good." Javier adjusted his Burberry tie and sipped from his bottle of Moët.

"When it comes to business, time is money, and you can't have both. It's either you have all the time in the world and no money, or you have all the money that you can possibly have and no time. You cannot have both." Rodolfo popped a Cert inside of his mouth. He believed in having fresh breath at all times. It was essential when doing business. Nobody wanted to have a business conversation with a person whose breath smelled like feces. He knew he didn't, and a person wouldn't believe how absolutely common it was in the business world. "I got a message from Martina, two days ago. She says they're struggling back home. I think I'm going to fly down and check on them. I miss Justina."

"Martina made it very clear when she found out about me that she didn't want anything else to do with you. She even threatened to kill you. Why are you chasing demons?" Javier didn't give two fucks about his father's first wife. She'd hated him ever since his mother, Geneva who was at a point and time Martina's best friend, exposed that she was, in fact,

Rodolfo's child's mother as well and that Javier was born five years before Rodolfo and Martina had their first child, Joaquin.

"Javier one thing you are going to learn about women is that they will say anything when they are angry or in the heat of the moment. They are very emotional, and impulsive when they are angry. You shouldn't hold weight to anything that they say during their anger outburst. Martina had a right to snap the way that she did. I fucked up a lot during our marriage. I kept secrets, I cheated, I ran the entire gambit. It's a wonder why she didn't kill me?"

Javier was bored with the topic already. "What about me. I am your firstborn and this woman hates my guts. Do you have any idea how that makes me feel?"

Rodolfo could only imagine. "Man up," he spat. "Besides Justina, and Joaquin are my children. Shouldn't I do for them as I do for you?"

"Martina will never accept your money. She hasn't done it in all these years, and she won't now. The fact that she called you is shocking to me. It's a cause for concern. You might not be worried, but you should be. The people of La Perla are snakes, and our family is no different."

Rodolfo glared at his son. "So, you think it is wise to leave them to struggle even after the storm has devastated so much of the island. What kind of man does that make me if I continue this charade of a pussy, huh?"

"She will never accept any help from you. You can try, and I wish you the best. That's all I can say."

"I have a major drop off to San Juan in a week and I am going to see them while I am down there. You are more than welcome to fly down with me."

Javier snickered. "For what? Not only are you flying with a hundred kilos of Heroin, but you're going to see a family that doesn't give two fucks about you. It makes no sense. Besides that day, I am throwing me a 'We Are Eighteen', pool party at the Kingdom Hotel. You have fun, I sure plan on having a good time."

Rodolfo shook his head. "I have sheltered and spoiled you way too much over these last years. It is my fault for making you cold-hearted and without compassion."

Sudan stepped into the boardroom escorted by two of Rodolfo's trained assassins that worked as bodyguards. She cleared her throat. "Excuse me but am I interrupting something?" She stopped at the side of Javier.

Javier stood up and took her hand. He kissed the back of it. "Damn, you get finer and finer every time I see you."

Sudan smiled at him for a moment, then dismissed him as only secondly important behind Rodolfo. She extended her hand to Rodolfo. "The name is Sudan and I am so happy to finally meet you."

Rodolfo knew a beautiful woman when he saw one, and Sudan was so beautiful to him that she left him awestruck. He took her hand and kissed the back of it three times. "The pleasure is all mine." He pulled out her seat and took his again. "To what do I owe the Sudanese government this honor?"

"We are interested in acquiring some very important land from you, Mr. Peralta, amongst other things of course." She batted her eyelashes at him.

"I assure you that any land I have you will not want. But go ahead and let me hear you out."

Sudan grabbed her laptop out of her Birkin bag and pulled up the map of La Perla, Puerto Rico. She turned the screen around so he could see it. "This land will be just for starters."

Rodolfo recognized La Perla immediately. He laughed. "Well, this is just La Perla. Nobody owns this other than the Puerto Rican government."

"And you and I both know who owns them." She chuckled. "However, I didn't come here to play games. We are willing to make you a hundred million dollars richer within the next ninety days. If you can facilitate and pave the way to have this expanse of shacks and concrete miniature homes torn down so that we can acquire this land and rebuild it into a resort. We are also willing to pay you a monthly royalty for each month that we accrue finances from our said resort for a period of fifty years. I'm thinking in addition to the hundred million dollars, you will see no less than fifty thousand dollars a month."

Rodolfo took a sip from his glass of Champagne. His eyes got bucked. "Those numbers sound amazing. Why La Perla, why now? It's mostly ruined, and on the edge of destruction."

"La Perla is still close to Paradise. Once we tear it down and rebuild it into a wealthy person's getaway, it will be the focal point of all vacations. It will be the summer's version of Aspen. We have major ideas for the region, and we need your help in spearheading these endeavors. What do you say?"

"Where is the pen, I'll sign for him," Javier joked seriously. He was hoping Rodolfo didn't squander the moment.

"Give me some time to think about this. It all sounds so fascinating, and easy. The Mayor and I are in an understanding. She is looking to enter politics and a resort-like place could afford her the right to hobnob and grease some palms with the right politicians. I am sure I can get this deal done. It's not a matter of if I can, just when. Is there a deadline?"

Sudan began typing away on her computer. "If you agree to set the wheels in motion. We are willing to pay you a hundred thousand dollars, right now. Also, we would like to cop some of your finest Heroin, and when this resort takes off, both your coke and your dog food will be what we use to supply our clientele. You have my word on that. In short, there is no room for you to lose. There will only be gains all across the board."

Rodolfo liked the sound of that, though his gut told him that whenever something sounded too good it usually was.

Sudan lowered her eyes. "These are the deals that we have on the table. Javier has my contact information. When you are ready to go, I will push a button and the money flow will start. Your net worth of three million will be immediately increased," she said this last part just to let Rodolfo know that she had researched him inside and out.

While he spent money sometimes frivolously, he was nothing more than an early millionaire, meaning that his millions did not surpass the five-million-dollar mark. He was small-time, and the Sudanese power players knew it.

Rodolfo swallowed his spit. "You have put a lot on my plate. I will make my rounds, then I will get back to you as soon as possible. In fact, I will be in La Perla within a week. Let me look some things over and see where we are. Is that a deal?"

Sudan stood up and nodded. "The sooner the better. My people are thirsty for success within the islands. Keep me informed." She snapped her fingers and headed out of the boardroom.

"Sudan we're still family on, right?" Javier couldn't help asking this question while looking at her ass. It was plump and juggled with each step she took. He could already imagine how pink her pussy would be.

"You help out your father in any way that you can to get this thing progressing, and I'll show some things you didn't even know women could do. I promise you that, bet."

Javier sat as he felt his penis telescoping from imagining what Sudan was like in the sack. "Bet, I'll be in touch."

***

Fancy opened the door to take out her garbage and was shocked to see Peto standing on her porch getting ready to knock on her door. She jumped back and pulled a tube of Mace from her right pocket, but then dropped it. She bent over to pick it up, and that's when Peto being at the door finally clicked in her mind. The threat assessment of him dropped to zero.

Peto laughed and picked it up for her. "Mamita, you're tripping. What were you doing to do, spray me?"

Fancy stood up and felt a sharp pain shoot through her lower back. It was that time of the month and she felt irritable. "Nall, you just caught me off guard that's all. What brings you here?"

"One second." Peto took the garbage from her and jogged across the parking lot. He tossed the big white plastic bag into the air. It landed in the metal dumpster. He jogged back and stopped in front of her as the sun began to set. "A'ight, I need to talk to you about Javier. He and Kelis are sleeping together and I am thinking about killing him and her. I need you to talk me out of it."

Fancy looked around. "Boy be quiet, Javier got all kinds of people around here listening and watching everything I do." She didn't know if it was the truth, but she figured it was. "Come inside." She continued to look around as if she were paranoid.

When they made it inside, she led him to the living room and made sure Vatican was busy on her iPad in the back room. She ordered her to not come out. Then she grabbed two beers and met Peto back in the living room. She handed him a brew. "Here, Peto, now tell me what's going on?"

"It's quite simple honestly." He popped the tab on the beer. "I caught them fuckin' at our house and doing some other shit in his truck. I didn't even know that she liked him. I bought this." He pulled a .45 off his waistband and set it on the table.

"Peto!" Fancy's eyes were as big as saucers as she looked over the gun. She saw that Peto meant business. It was exciting to her as much as she hated to admit it. "What are you planning on doing with that?"

"I wanna shoot him until that gun starts clicking symbolizing that it's empty. The Bible says that a husband's wrath over somebody violating his wife will be deadly. Why should I not follow it? I love Kelis." He drank the entire can of Beer in less than thirty seconds.

Fancy had to think about things logically. She had been trying to find a way to get rid of Javier ever since they had both picked Vatican up from school four days ago, and nothing came to her mind. Now that Peto was jaded and already planning on killing Javier she thought it was in her best interest to make the situation work for her. After all, she wanted Javier out of the picture by any means. Javier being deceased meant she could use Vatican to continue to get funds out of Rodolfo. He was obsessed with Vatican, the only culprit that stood in the way of hers and Vatican's imminent and long-term happiness was Javier.

Fancy tried to calm down her giddiness. She got up and sat beside Peto. He smelled bad his funk made her stomach churn. "Peto, you know the only reason Kelis is stepping out on you is because Javier is waving money around in her face. She loves you but as long as he is alive and doing that, he is going to destroy your family. Now I have known you longer than him, and I owe you my loyalty. I think we need to come up with a plan to get rid of him."

Peto looked over at her shaking from anger. "You would do that for me?"

Fancy nodded. "I love you, Peto, and I feel you and Kelis are meant to be. I will help you get rid of him. We will come up with a plan. Family is everything."

Peto stood up, he was shaking worse than ever. "If you do this, I promise I will be ready to die for you."

Fancy lowered her eyes, she felt powerful. Mental manipulation was everything. She felt that it was a woman's strongest tool. "Peto, I will be honored to help you. You are my brother. Now hug me." The sadistic wheels began to turn in her head as she held him. Javier was living on borrowed time.

Chapter 8

"Joaquin, Joaquin, open the door!" Justina beat on Joaquin's door over and over. La Perla was experiencing a heatwave, and she had sweat sliding down the sides of her face, and under her arms. She felt sticky and oddly uncomfortable. She bawled her fists tighter and beat on Joaquin's door again. "Open up! I know you hear me pounding on this damn door?"

Joaquin pulled the door open. He looked rough and rugged. His face was unwashed, his curls were all over the place, and he felt depleted. He rubbed his eyes. "Justina, why are you beating on my door like you're crazy? Can't you see that I'm in here trying to get my thoughts together?"

"Daddy is here. He just texted me that he has landed at Roberto Clemente Airport. He'll be here in a few hours, I can't wait. I'm so excited. You look like shit, get it together." She turned to run away from him.

He grabbed her arm. "Wait, Rodolfo is coming here? Who okayed this? I know that my mother didn't." He ran his hand over his face to try and wake up. He felt sluggish, and a bit dizzy.

"Mama is the one that called him. She's tired of us struggling especially when we don't have to. So, daddy is coming to save the day and I am so happy. You should be too."

"This man has left us to fend for ourselves for years on end. Now that he has remembered he has a family you act like you're about to meet the Pope. What is the matter with you?"

Justina yanked her arm away from him. "You're the only one that has a problem with our father, not me? I don't care about his other son or any other kids that he has. He's rich, and he can take our family out of this poverty. We need him. It's as simple as that."

"We don't need him. We've been doing just fine without him." Joaquin felt insulted. He couldn't stand the thought of being in the same city as Rodolfo, let alone the same house.

"Your stubbornness toward Papi has made you stupid. We are poor and destitute. There is no reason for it. If mama can forgive him, then you must as well. She is dying of cancer, though. But I don't think she's told you that yet." Justina walked off and left him frozen in place.

Martina stepped out of the shadows. "Joaquin, we need to talk."

Joaquin was still stuck from the news Justina had uttered to him. He turned to face Martina. "Mama, tell me it's not true? Tell me you don't have cancer, and that you didn't invite this man to come from America to save us."

"Joaquin, first of all, you need to calm down. You're getting yourself riled up over things that you cannot change. Now come with me so we can sit down in the living room and talk like civilized adults." She snapped her fingers. "Let's go."

Joaquin lowered his head and slowly followed her commands. He was the first to sit. "What kind of cancer, Mama?"

"Cervical, I've been battling it for a while, and every time it goes away it comes back again. It's spread this time pretty severely the doctors are saying that there is nothing that they can do."

"Again, and there is nothing that they can do? Mama, I didn't even know you had it the first time. Why didn't you tell me?" He felt himself becoming emotional. 'Not Martina, not my mother. What will I do without her?' was the constant thought that traveled through his mind.

"I didn't tell nobody because it ain't nobody's business other than my own. The only reason your sister found out is because she was rummaging through my things. She's nosey and that's no good. But that's neither here nor there. The doctors gave me three months to live.

Joaquin fell off the couch, to her feet. He hugged her waist. "No! No! Mama please not you!" Tears came sailing down his cheeks. He hugged her tighter.

Martina was the second to become wildly emotional. "There is no need for me to leave you children behind to struggle when you have a father that is rich and powerful. I am willing to tuck my tail and submit to him so that you two can have a relationship with your second parent. We need help, and we need to get a better footing in La Perla. We're so poor," her voice got low.

Joaquin made his way to his feet. "We don't need his help, Mama, and you don't need to bow down to him. I will make things happen for us. Please just trust me. How much will it cost to get you more time on this earth with us? Tell me please." He wiped the tears from his eyes.

Martina stood in front of his face. "I have a three month old son, that's it. Even with the best doctors in the world, the most I can get is a year, if even that."

Joaquin pulled her to him and hugged her as tight as he could. "No woman or no man on this earth means more to me than you do. You are my life. I will never recover if I lose you." He stepped back and looked in her face. "Mama, I'm telling you, if I lose you, I will become a lunatic. My heart will become as cold as ice. It is only you that keeps me grounded. Nobody else." He held her shaking because he felt himself turning mildly psychotic.

Martina took ahold of his face in her hands. "Hush, little baby, you are strong. I will never leave you, Joaquin. I will only become a part of your soul, and from there I will protect your heart. Do you understand me?" She kissed both of his cheeks, then his lips. Her face went from smiling to that of anger.

"However, if you ever decide to take out that deep-seated anger and hatred that lives inside of you, make sure you direct it at our Mayor. Cruz is corrupt, and she's been looking to sell out our people from the moment she got in office. They all want to do away with La Perla, but you stop them. This is our land, and La Perla is my home. I was born here, and I will die here. When they put me in the ground, I will rest in peace knowing that La Perla is guarded by the fury of my son. Only then will I be able to rest in peace.

"You will be the King of this island. I can feel it in my heart, and right here in my stomach." Her face was a mask of anger. "Your father is going to help the Mayor sell us out. He's looking to buy up La Perla and sell it to foreigners. You stop him." She hissed. "This is our homeland." She held the right side of his face in her hand.

Joaquin nodded feeling himself becoming heated with ambition. "How, Mama? How do I stop all of this from happening?"

"It's in your heart, baby. Follow your heart," as she finished these words Rodolfo began knocking on the front door to the shack.

"Daddy's here! Daddy's here!" Justina screamed running to the door in a pair of white biker shorts that were way too small for her.

"Remember, Joaquin, follow your heart." Martina hugged him tightly.

Joaquin kissed her forehead and released her. "I will, Mama, I promise." He rushed into his room and grabbed a pillowcase from his dresser. He filled it with three of his firearms and hurried out of the back door with Martina's words flowing heavily in his mind.

**

Five hours later Joaquin was sliding a pair of pantyhose over his face and cocking his trusted Mach .11 with murder on his mind if it needed to be that. He ducked down on the side of the Cigar shop with his heart pounding in his chest. Martina had been descriptive about his father's intended actions. She knew who he was supposed to be meeting with, but she couldn't tell Joaquin the exact amount of product or money that was supposed to be exchanged?

He didn't need it, all he needed to know was that he was hitting his father where it hurt and that after the big score he would be able to have a few finances that would help him and his family survive until he could figure things out for the future. The last thing he needed was Rodolfo rolling in and thinking he was about to play God and Savior for the Peralta's. Joaquin would have rather been hit by a train.

Joaquin looked to his right and then his left. The sounds of three people laughing emanated in his ears. Somebody broke a glass bottle. A woman screamed from her boyfriend tickling her on their way into the local bar. Joaquin stayed as low as he could to the ground and ran down the expanse of the alleyway until he came behind a candle shop. He stopped and peeked around the corner of the small garage that held motorbikes for deliveries.

There were two heavy-set men out back acting as lookouts. Joaquin took a deep breath and blew out his fear of the unknown. He slowly eased into the yard with a serrated US Army knife that Rodolfo had left behind when he fled in a haste to America after the Hurricane and his enemies became too great for him to handle. He crept as fast as he could, thankful that the men had their backs turned.

The taller, heavier set of the two turned toward the alley and blew a cloud of smoke toward the air. He squinted his eyes at the sound of Joaquin trekking across the grass. When he zoomed into the deadly Joaquin it was too late. He reached for his gun, and Joaquin pounced and jumped in the air with the knife in his hand. When he came down, he slammed the knife directly into the first man's heart and yanked it downward. He groaned and squeezed his eyes tight. His heart burst as he fell backward dead before the back of his head hit the grass.

Joaquin yanked the knife out of him and chased the other man who began to retreat for ten paces. He caught him quickly and slammed the blade into his neck. He fell to his knees. Joaquin kicked him in the back and knocked him forward. He sat on his waist and stabbed him over and over with a blank stare. His eyes were unblinking, he was in a murderous zone. He finished the man and stood up. He looked around, all appeared quiet. He got low once again and crept to the back of the candle shop.

***

Rodolfo stuffed the last of the million dollars into the tenth duffel bag and tossed it into the Pizza delivery van. Across the table, from him, Vinny was zipping close his twelfth duffel bag that was filled with Vietnamese Heroin. Rodolfo smiled and closed the door to his van.

"You've come a long way, Vinny. It seems like the last time I saw you, you were nothin' more than a peasant. Now you're putting together a million dollars, I'm proud of you."

Vinny laughed. "Yeah, well, you'd be surprised at how much Hurricane Maria changed everybody." He did the signal and gave the order for the three Jackers that he'd bought along with him to pick up the duffel bags.

"Well, it was nice doing business with you son. I'll see you in three months when you're finished flooding the island." Rodolfo turned to leave.

Vinny snickered. "Hey, Papi, about you walking away with my money. I don't know about that." He pulled a Desert Eagle with a beam out of his coat pocket and placed the red aimer right on Rodolfo's forehead.

Rodolfo cursed under his breath. "Son of a bitch, I shoulda known I couldn't trust you, Vinny. And that's why I didn't." Rodolfo fell to the floor.

Joaquin came from the side door with the Mach .11 in his hand and got to bucking like a maniac with extreme precision and aim, catching Vinny and his threesome off guard.

Boom! Boom! Boom! Boom!

Vinny caught two to the chest and fell backward. He bussed three times at Joaquin before he jumped up and got to running for his life. Joaquin popped him in the back twice. Vinny ran out the backdoor. Joaquin began to chop down the three remaining killas from Vinny's crew. He murdered two of them with neck and headshots. They twisted and landed on the pavement with blood spurting out of them.

The third one ran toward Rodolfo and was about to jump out of the garage where Rodolfo's rented pizza van was when Rodolfo slipped the .380 out of his boot and popped him three times under his chin. The bullets entered his throat and knocked massive chunks out of the back of his head. His brains fell to the pavement before his body did.

Rodolfo laid on his back. He threw the gun across the floor. "I'm unarmed, you can have the money, and you can have the drugs. They are yours. Just leave me with my life, please." Rodolfo knew it was Joaquin. He had been loose with his details for Martina. He knew they would make it back to his son.

Joaquin walked up on Rodolfo with hatred in his heart. He wanted to murder him for leaving them after the hurricane. He wanted to take his life for making them suffer, but the man in him couldn't and wouldn't allow him to murder his own father. "Get up and run," he hissed. "You got five seconds."

Rodolfo only needed two. "Thank you." He broke camp with a smile on his face.

***

That night Joaquin crept to Emilia's window at three-thirty in the morning. He tapped on it until she stuck her head out. Before she could speak, he cut her off by holding up a hand. "It's a new day in La Perla. Tonight, I announce myself as La Perla's new King. I love you, and your future is to be my wife." He turned away from her and left without looking back one time.

Chapter 9

"Javier, I promised you that if your father jumped on board with us, I would make your wildest dreams come true, and I meant every word I spoke to you." Sudan looked over at Javier while seated in the Private Jet. She took the glass of Chardonnay and sipped from it leaving red bubbly fizz around the rim of it.

Javier sat back and molded himself to the soft leather. He took a long swallow from the bottle of Moët, which was his favorite Champagne, and nodded his head. "My Pops always tell me that with everything you must have patience. I told you that it would take a few weeks to get everything up and going and that it would happen when it was supposed to. Now La Perla is for the Sudanese. It'll all work out in the end." He laughed and looked down at the bit of chocolate thigh Sudan was exposing.

She was wearing a very short white Prada skirt that exposed a lot of skin. He found himself barely able to contain himself. She was so sexy and black. For him, a night with her would be a sexual dream come true.

"Well, it isn't as easy as you're making it seem. We understand that there will be some intense rebellion from some other locals. But they are poor and destitute. It is the richer of the fighters that always win the war. We are looking to throw at them everything we have in order to bring La Perla under our grasp. Mayor Cruz will be the last obstacle. Once she is subdued and bought out, we will be free to invade La Perla. I feel sorry for those that are current residents there. Our first order of business will be to get the police force on board. Once they are the citizens will be at our mercy, and murder is our way of communication." She raised her right shoulder slightly and took another sip from her Wine.

"Sounds like it's going to suck for those that are still there. Lucky for me and my family we are here in America." He thought about Martina, and his half-siblings under her care. He felt nothing.

Martina had never accepted him, and he wished the worst fate imaginable for her. They were possible heirs to his father's estate. Javier wanted it all. He didn't want to split a dime with Joaquin and Justina. The thought felt like an insult to him. Javier was all about himself. Always had been, and he felt he always would be.

Sudan crossed her thick thighs and leaned into his personal space. The subtle scent of her perfume was intoxicating. She licked her juicy red painted lips. "What do you have in mind for me? Such an African goddess like myself, I wanna know." She brushed her nose from side to side on him.

Javier was forced to look cross-eyed at her in order to zoom into her eyes. "I'm 'bout what you're bout. This body doesn't intimidate me, it arouses me. As soon as this plane lands we're going to get to it." He placed his hand on her thigh.

Sudan's bodyguards that were sitting in the back of them took pistols from their waists and pressed it to the back of Javier's head. Both hammers were cocked, one wrapped an arm around Javier's neck, while the other pressed his pistol to Javier's temple. They hadn't heard Sudan give Javier permission to touch her, and that was a no-no.

Sudan grunted, and held up a hand. "It's okay, let him go. We are merely flirting."

Javier was released. He rubbed his neck and looked back at them with mounting anger. "Muthafuckas, don't you see her flirting with me as well?"

The two Sudanese bodyguards ignored him and sat staring over Javier's shoulder. Their job was to protect Sudan at all costs. Nothing Javier said was going to change that. They held their pistols in their right hands and remained poised for attack.

Javier rubbed the back of his neck. "Damn, you gotta admire their discipline, though."

Sudan grabbed him by the shirt and brought his lips to hers. "I ain't never been with a Spanish man before. Is it as passionate as they make it seem in the books?" She licked his lips.

Javier tried to catch her tongue with his lips. His eyes gazed down at her thighs again. Now the skirt had ridden up to the point that it was sitting in her lap. Her red see-through panties were displayed. He could make out her sexy thick chocolate pussy lips. He wanted to rub them, as soon as the thought crossed his mind though he remembered the two angry-looking Black Gorillas behind him.

"When do we land?" His dick was harder than Calculus.

Sudan reached into his lap and squeezed it. She purred into his ear and opened her thighs wider. The crotch of her panties trapped itself between her sex lips and puffed them outward. Her labia was engorged, she was aroused, and ready to show Javier a thing or two. She sucked his ear lobe.

"We land in fifteen minutes. Do you think you'll be able to keep your hands off me until then?" She tried to pump his dick through his pants.

Javier began to shake, he wanted Sudan so bad. "Hell n'all, but I ain't got no other choice. Man, can I do something? Tell your henchmen to leave me alone and you let me get to it."

Sudan giggled sexily. "Those henchmen are my brothers, and they've been given their orders. Now, do you want to see what I taste like?" She pulled her panties to the side showing him her cleft. Her middle finger ran up and down her slit opening herself up for him. She wiped her finger on his bottom lip.

Javier sucked it into his mouth and savored the flavor of Sudan. "Can I touch you? Will they let me?" He was dying to be all up in her personal places.

She looked back at her security and gave them the eye to let Javier be. "Go ahead, you can touch me."

Before she could finish the sentence good enough, Javier's mouth was attached to her pussy. He forced his tongue deep into her and darted it in and out at full speed, then he was sucking on her clitoris while he held her ass cheeks in his hands. His nose bumped all over her clit driving her crazy. Her taste was addicting to him. He'd popped two pink Mollies and the drug was coursing through his system only adding to his arousal and sexual wantonness.

Sudan turned toward him and placed her right ankle on the back of the seat. Her red bottom was in the air. She wanted to give Javier all the access he needed to get her right. She held her lips open for him. He licked her fingers while at the same time attacking her pussy like it was going to be his last chance at getting any for the rest of his life. Sudan moaned and scooted closer to his tongue.

Javier slurped and held her lips open. "When do we land? I wanna fuck this black ass pussy. You're so wet, I can feel with my tongue how tight you are. I need to be in this pussy already. Mmm." He slid his tongue into her and fucked it in and out at full speed while his nose played with her clitoris. The erect bud leaked her secretions onto him. Her scent began to fill the small plane. Even her security guards were erect and finding it uncomfortable to avoid adjusting themselves.

Sudan gripped the seat and looked into the back seat just as her head bodyguard took his dick and moved it to a more comfortable position inside his pants. It still stuck upward. She trembled and came humping into Javier's mouth.

"Uhhh! Uhhhh! Uhhhh!" she hollered.

***

Peto paced back and forth inside of his living room. He had a bulletproof vest across his chest, and a mind full of anger and heartache. Kelis came into the living room and stopped in her tracks. She had Alexis on her hip. She bounced her up and down and looked Peto over suspiciously. Something told her that he was going through a mental battle and that he wasn't in his right mind. She slowly backed out of the living room after seeing his .45 on the table. There were bullets that needed to be loaded into the gun all over the table.

"Peto, is everything okay?" She asked turning sideways so that the side that Alexis was on was pointed away from the danger that was him.

Peto stopped pacing and stared at her with glossy eyes. He was hopped on cocaine and pain pills. "I just need to know if you love me? If you do, that we will be together despite our struggles. I need to know you will always choose me over any other man no matter how much money he has. Please tell me this, Kelis. Please!" He came over to her and took a hold of her blouse.

Kelis smacked his hand away. She could smell the alcohol on his breath. "You're drunk. How dare you come into this house drunk and armed to the teeth with artillery? Your daughter lives here."

"Is she my daughter? Tell me if Alexis is mine? Or does she belong to somebody else?"

Kelis was shocked and dismayed. "You took my virginity. How dare you question her paternity after so many months? What's gotten into you?"

Peto snatched the gun off the table. "I love you, Kelis, and I love her. I would never hurt you the way you hurt me. I can't take this shit." He swiped the bullets into the palm of his hand and stormed out of the house slamming the door behind him.

Kelis was so confused. It never crossed her mind that Peto knew about her and Javier. She simply thought he was hopped up on drugs, and she felt terrible for him. "I have to get you away from that man, Alexis. You deserve safety and comfort. Things that Peto can't provide you, or me for that matter." She kissed her baby and got up from the couch. She was ready to leave Peto behind. It was time, she thought. Life had to be more than what Peto could offer her and Alexis.

***

"Look at me baby, don't pay attention to the Lions. They are only here for my protection. They will not harm you." Sudan walked up to Javier with her red satin Negligee. It was covered by a short robe that was basically pointless in the covering of her. Her body was clearly visible underneath it and it had Javier thirsty to be inside her. The room was grand. It had big, all-white pillows, and soft white, silk sheets. The bed was custom made. There were two king-sized beds placed together. To the left of the bed was a shallow pool with blue mouthwash colored water inside it. A roaring fireplace was on the right side of the massive bed and pacing around the bed were two huge Lionesses that had been imported from Africa. Sudan had both female Lions ever since she was two years old. They were what Americans considered to be their dogs, and they were freaking Javier out.

"Sudan, why don't you put them in a cage or somethin'? They don't need to be in here now."

Sudan nearly took offense to his comments. "You are never supposed to cage a female or a woman of any sort. These Lionesses are my spirits, and while I am connecting

80

with you, they will feel me spiritually. Now come, Papi. " She opened her short robe and dropped it to the floor. She walked closer to Javier until she was in his embrace. Her right hand took hold of his dick again. This time she found it limp. She was disgusted. "Are you not interested in what you see before you? Or are you so much of a wimp that the sight of my spirits has stolen your manhood away?" She grew angry.

One of the huge Lionesses walked closely to Javier and sniffed his air. She could sense his fear and it made her stomach growl. She began to look at him as prey, and a possible meal. Sudan had been feeding her the flesh of her enemies ever since the Lionesses were cubs. The Lioness rubbed up against the other Lioness and gave her a signal that Javier was potential food for them both to devour. Their eyes became low and trained on his jugular.

Javier couldn't focus on anything other than the Lions. "Sudan, you're fine as a muthafucka baby. I wanna do this body justice but I ain't never been around no Lions before. This shit is blowing me, right now. Can you please put them up?"

"Fear is something that can be sensed by animals but not by humans. Fear comes when a man or a woman are unsure of their surroundings, and they look to flee in order to seek protection. In order to be a true King, or a conquer, fear needs to be absent from a person's mind frame. When it comes to doing business with outsiders of Sudan our business associates must be fearless because our government takes risks that most are petrified to take. So, Javier, are you a bitch, or are you a man?" she screamed.

The Lionesses slowly crept toward them and stepped onto the bed where Sudan stood on her knees a few paces from Javier.

Javier began to sweat. The closer the Lions got, the more worried he became. "Man, I-I-I'm a man from Sudan. What the fuck is going on? Get these animals out of the bed."

Sudan stood up. "These are not animals. They are my spirits, and you have five minutes to change the feeling in my spirit before you become dinner."

Chapter 10

Joaquin ran at full speed, he panted and tried to control his breathing. His toes dug into the earth and thrust upward to allow him to run faster and faster. The Mach .90 in his hands threw off the rhythm of his sprint but he was dead set on mastering it. The rain poured down harder and harder with each step he took, lightning flashed brightly. His clothes were matted to him. He got to the edge of the hill and rolled down it over and over. Behind him, his crew of La Perla Mambas did the same.

There was no beef that they were retreating from, they were simply getting used to the elements of their land that Joaquin had sworn to protect by any means necessary. They slid down the muddy hill that overlooked El Morro, and the Governor's mansion of the island. When they came to the bottom of it, Joaquin stood with mud dripping off him. The wind blew harshly as the loud thunder boomed overhead. His troops landed and got up to stand behind him. They were thirty deep and pledged their undying loyalty to Joaquin who had taken a nice portion of the money that he'd robbed from Rodolfo to pay all their families' bills and to put food into their shacks and pockets.

Pedro stood beside him with fire in his eyes. Though his tongue had been taken at Joaquin's behest Pedro felt as if he owed Joaquin his life for sparing his own. He placed his hand on Joaquin's shoulder, then looked about at the Governor's mansion. He clutched his Mach .90 in silence.

Joaquin turned around to address his crew of bloodthirsty, island protecting savages. The rain seemed to pick up with fierce velocity. "They want to take our land from us! They say that this land is garbage and that it needs to be torn down so that they can build a resort on it. Damn, the countless Puerto

Ricans that have been born here, that have fought here, struggled here and died here. We mean nothin' to them!"

Lightning flashed across the sky. The crew of angry savages kept their silence, but the rage deep within them began to mount. The wind whistled; lightning struck the water four hundred yards in front of them. But all were focused on Joaquin. The weather and its elements meant nothing.

"We are from La Perla! This is our home! This is our land! We must be willing to suffer for this land. We must be willing to shed blood, a lot of it! We must be willing to die for La Perla! Sacrifices must come daily in order to sustain what we know rightfully belongs to us. We are a family. You are my blood. My blood is La Perla!" He stood with his chest heaving up and down. He turned to look out at the Governor's mansion across the water. He kept silent for a full five minutes. He lowered his head.

Then he turned back around to face his brethren. "Mayor Cruz has sold us out. Those that took oaths to protect our people are doing the opposite. We are alone! We are alone but strong. All we have is each other. It is La Perla against the world. My name is, Joaquin, and I stand here because I am ready to die for the sake of our land. If you are as well then you will hold me up high as your king. Your king of La Perla. I will not fail you. I will meet death before that happens. So, my brethren which of you are really with me?" He stepped forward ten paces. "If you are then come stand behind me."

One by one the crew of savages began to come and stand behind him until there were only twelve left remaining on the other side. The rain was coming down so hard that it was difficult for any that were present to attain clear visibility. Joaquin glared at the remaining members that had not chosen to stand behind him.

A slender, short male stepped forward. "Mayor Cruz is corrupt. She is connected with a lot of white people in America. When the uprising begins, she will be quick to annihilate all that oppose her. How will you protect us all? How will we fight against her and live to see past the day that she attacks with her military of marksmen?"

"We are fighting to die! But we are doing it on our terms. We will not allow Cruz to take this land away from us without us wreaking havoc on her and her entire establishment. What you see here is not the end result, it is only the beginning. Now are you with us or not?" Spoke another one of the men.

Ten more of the remaining savages left to stand behind Joaquin. Only two remained standing.

The slender male spit on the ground. "I think all of you are out of your minds. La Perla isn't worth all of this. You fools will rot in hell more sooner than later. You can count me out." He turned around to leave but wound up bumping into a hooded Emilia. She had been the last savage left standing.

"If you will not stand for Joaquin, then you are against La Perla." She took a step back and raised her Mach before she pulled the trigger shredding the man's head into twenty pieces. It was a bloody explosion. He fell to his knees lifeless. Emilia stepped over him and stood in front of Joaquin. "I'm with you, my king. So, what's next?"

Joaquin stared across the waters again at the Governor's mansion. "Next we let them know that we are here, and we aren't going anywhere anytime soon."

***

Martina stirred the spicy pot of sauce and hummed to herself a melodious tune. She picked the wooden spoon up from the pot and tasted her mixture of herbs and spices. She nodded her head in approval. She went back to stirring and side-stepped to grab the pound of ground beef from the counter when she felt an icy chill go down her spine. When she turned around a ski-masked Vinny was holding Justina with his arm around her throat. He placed the blade to her face and sneered at Martina.

Martina was an old Puerto Rican at heart. She understood war and knew that this had to be an act of it. "Why are you in my home? And what are you doing to my daughter?" she asked calmly.

This threw Vinny off, he tightened his grip on Justina. "Your son has somethin' that belongs to me. I want it back or the two of you will become my targets until you are deceased."

Martina added a dash of Cayenne Peppers to her dish. She looked back at Vinny and laughed. "A man that looks to target women instead of the man that he is warring with is nothing more than a coward. You are only targeting us because you feel that we are inferior to you by gender." She tasted the sauce again. Now it was banging, she added the ground beef, and stirred it slowly.

Vinny thought that she was obviously out of her mind. "Bitch if you think I'm playing with you I will kill your daughter, right here and right now." He pulled upward with his arms and exposed Justina's neck. He pressed the blade to it and began to cut enough for Justina to draw blood.

Justina closed her eyes, she didn't fear death. Both Joaquin and Martina had taught her early in the beginning that death was a natural part of life. You couldn't avoid it, and you couldn't determine when your time was about to come but when it came you were to accept it and make peace.

Martina turned the fire up on her sauce. It bubbled and popped at her. The heat is what made the spices seep evenly through the meat, so it was necessary. "What are you looking for from myself, and my daughter? We have nothin' to do with your war with my child. We are merely innocent and women of the shack. We rarely leave our home for any reason."

Vinny moved his front around on Justina's pert backside. The feel of its softness was causing him to become aroused. He'd caught her changing clothes, so she stood in nothing more than a pair of thin white panties that were too small for her. Her cheeks were exposed on each side. "I want you to contact your son, and to tell him to bring me my dope and the money that he stole from Rodolfo."

Martina smiled. "Rodolfo is Joaquin's father. Why would he steal anything from him when he could ask for it?"

"Because your son is a low down, no good, snake that thinks he owns La Perla. But he will soon find out that there are bigger sharks in the water than him. Now bitch, when will he be back?"

"Justina, you know I love you, and you are my heart. This man has come to kill us, and since we are nothin' more than defenseless women I guess we might as well let him. I mean, after all, men are superior to women, aren't they baby?"

"No, ma'am." Justina swallowed her spit.

"Awe, baby, but sure they are. If they weren't then why would I have to use this!" She picked up the pot of boiling hot sauce and dished it into Vinny's face.

Vinny could feel his skin peeling off from the intense heat. He released Justina and fell backward against the refrigerator screaming in pain like a character in a horror movie. He smacked at himself to get the sauce off him. "You bitch!" He struggled to see.

Justina appeared from the pantry with a baseball bat. She raised it over her head and brought it down as hard as she could busting his cranium wide open. Blood spurt across the stove. "I am a woman." She clunked him a second time knocking another chunk out of his head.

"Arrgh!" Vinny was in a pushup position.

Martina came out of her bedroom with a loaded double-barrel shotgun just as Joaquin was coming into the shack. She slammed it to the back of Vinny's head and sat on his back. "You prey on the weak and you will find them to be the strongest. Long live La Perla."

Boom!

Vinny's brains splashed across the floor in baby bits of bloody noodles. The brain matter had smoke that emitted from it. He lay blinking his eyes for a full minute. Joaquin stepped over him and stomped his face as hard as he could with his muddy boots, then Vinny faded away to death.

***

That night Joaquin, Justina, and Martina sat on the kitchen floor with plastic beneath them cutting Vinny into little bitty pieces of Shark food. They ate the Spanish lasagna that Martina had put together, and laughed happily, reminiscing about old times. Joaquin had never felt closer to his family. He silently swore to protect them for the rest of his life, no matter what it would take.

Chapter 11

The black Mercedes Benz van sped down the side of Park Avenue and slammed on its brakes. Smoke emitted from the tires, while a loud screeching resonated from the rubber skidding across the tar-covered road. The side door opened, and Javier was tossed out of it. He landed in the middle of the street, then he rolled for five yards before he came to a stop at Rodolfo's Maury Gator shoes. The van sped away again, one of the animals inside closed the door back.

Rodolfo bent down and pulled the duct tape off Javier's mouth. "How many times will I have to save you before my power and prestige is ignored?" He cut Javier's binds with his pocket knife.

Javier jumped up and ripped the rest of the tape off himself. He tossed it carelessly to the street. "That bitch had two Lions inside her bedroom, and she made it seem like it was normal. Then she turned on me when I couldn't perform." He spit on the concrete. "That's the last time I trust an African whore." He rubbed his wrists.

Rodolfo didn't know what to make of Javier. At times he felt so disappointed with his oldest son. He yearned for a relationship with Joaquin but he felt as if it was already tarnished because he had left Joaquin, Justina, and Martina behind to pursue business ventures in America after Martina found out that Rodolfo had an older illegitimate son by the name of Javier.

"Javier, soon you will be in charge of the empire I am building. Yet you have not shown me any signs that you are ready to do so. What am I to do as your father?"

Javier dusted himself off. "Shid I don't know, I guess you're supposed to be a dad and prepare me to do what I need to do in order to take over the Empire from you. What is the matter?"

Rodolfo walked away from Javier, opened the door to his fire red Rafe, and got in. He stepped on the gas. "Let's go, Javier. I have business to attend to. It seems pointless to stand here trying to reason with you when you have no sense of understanding of what I'm even getting at."

Javier mugged his father's whip, then pointed at him. "You might not like the man that I am but I'm the only son you have that gives a flying fuck about you! Now I made a mistake. I chased the wrong kind of pussy all the way to Sudan, and she shitted on. Turn the page!"

Rodolfo jerked his head back. "Excuse me?" He stepped out of the car and took off his suit jacket. He flung it on the back seat and walked over to Javier unbuttoning the sleeves of his shirt.

Javier was irritated. "What are you doing all of that for?"

A car rolled past them and kept going. They were on a dark street that was illuminated sparsely by a few street lamps.

"When I was a boy growing up in South Africa with my father before we migrated to Puerto Rico, he taught me two very important things. The first, a man should never swear, or speak ill around his parents unless he hates them or has no respect for them or what they stand for. Secondly, if a man does swear and speak ill while his father is present, he must be willing to suffer the consequences. Therefore, you must be ready to accept them?"

"What?" Javier was still confused.

Rodolfo walked up to Javier and punched him as hard as he could in the jaw knocking his son back five paces. The punch rang loudly in the night. Rodolfo threw up his fists and held his guard at chin level. "Support your filthy mouth, with your foul language. The next blow will come through your teeth."

Javier held his face in shock, his anger set in. He bounced off the car that he'd been leaning against and made haste to get back to Rodolfo. "How dare you put your fuckin' hands on me?"

Rodolfo held his guards closed to his chin. As soon as Javier got close enough again, he hit him in the mouth with his right hand and pivoted on his left toe. Blood spurt from his lips, Rodolfo felt no remorse. "Let's go!"

Javier had never been a scrapper. It was one of the reasons he kept a gun on him at all times for moments such as these. He spit blood on to the ground. "Papi, you're tripping man. We're supposed to be family."

"All you care about is you, Javier. You were even against me helping your brother and sister back in La Perla. That told me everything I need to know about you as a father. The lavish lifestyle has made you selfish, and inconsiderate. I do not recognize you as my son as much as I would love to. I am this close to cutting you off and establishing a relationship with Joaquin. His heart is full of compassion and empathy for others outside of himself. Something that you know nothing about."

"You love Joaquin more than me, just say it. I am your firstborn son. Your heir, and because I do not come from Martina, your first love, I will never be as good as Joaquin in your sight. Neither Justina either, admit it! This is why you have caused me to bleed, isn't it?" he hollered with anger sizzling inside of him.

Rodolfo took a deep breath and sighed. "Javier, you deserved what you got because you are disrespectful and have no sense of sacred boundaries when it comes to me. No man is ever supposed to swear by heaven or by earth in front of his father. You don't give me my honest due. It has nothing to do with my love for Joaquin and Justina."

"Lies! You don't care about me. You never have. You've only brought me with you when I was a little boy out of guilt, not love. You have always been ice cold to me. Always treated me as if I were only your stepchild and not your son. I'm not stupid, and I don't care anymore. But when you say that I treat you a certain way. You should really ask yourself why that is?" Javier waved him off. "Get lost, I'll find my own way home.

Rodolfo allowed him to get a quarter block away before he called out to him. "Javier! Javier! My son! Get back here, right now! Javier!"

Javier ignored his father, with each step that he took his heart became colder and colder. The love that he once had for his old man disappeared and a deep-seated hatred settled in its place. He hated his siblings, even more, especially Joaquin. He wanted to destroy his brother. He was sure his father never spoke about him the way he spoke highly of Joaquin. Javier nodded his head in intense anger as he walked through the dark streets.

'Because of the old man one day soon I will make Joaquin, and Justina pay. Martina is already being handled by God.' He thought about the revelation of her cancer diagnosis and snickered. "Bitches get what they deserve. She could never be better than my mother," he said out loud.

***

Fancy was snapped out of her sleep by the sounds of Javier going through her refrigerator. She slid out of the bed and grabbed a baseball bat that was resting up against it. She slipped on her robe and tied the sash to it as tight as she could.

Then she slowly eased out of the room. She hadn't used more than five steps before she spotted Javier standing in the middle of the kitchen with a beer in his hand. She breathed a sigh of relief, thankful that he was not an intruder.

Javier looked up and saw Fancy easing into the kitchen. "Damn, Mami, did I wake you?"

"Javier, what is going on? Why are you here?" She peeked down the hallway to see if Vatican's door was open when she saw that it wasn't; it brought her a sense of comfort.

"I just got into a fight with my old man. He hit me a couple of times and now I'm trying to keep from killing his ass." He held the bottle of beer up to his busted lip, and then to his eye that was slightly swollen.

"Okay, but you're still not explaining why you're here. You've never just popped up without calling first. What if I had company?"

Javier ignored her questioning. "My father said, I was selfish. He said that I only care about myself. I need to know if you think the same way?"

Fancy saw that she wasn't about to get anywhere with Javier until she addressed what was going on inside of him. The sooner they addressed it the faster he would be out of her home. "No, Javier, I don't think you are selfish. I think you are just annoyingly headstrong. You will do for people, but later down the line whatever you do for them you throw it back in their faces. That's not selfish."

Javier stared blankly at her as if he was trying to process what she'd just said to him. "Well, I don't mean to be selfish. I will give a person my last." He took hold of Fancy's hand and pulled her into the Den. He made her sit on the white leather sofa. He was drunk and high off Cocaine mixed with Marijuana. "I hadn't been the greatest baby daddy to you. You do a great job with our working daughter and I need to give you more credit." He pulled out twenty thousand dollars wrapped in rubber bands. "Here, this is for you." He tossed the three bundles of cash to her. They were in all small faced hundreds.

Fancy caught the money and looked at him as if he was crazy. She stood back up. "Javier, what is the matter with you? Why are you giving me all these funds?"

He pulled out a laced blunt and sparked it. "I got all that money put up, and my old man just closed in on a major deal with a bunch of Africans. There is no need for me to have all the cash that I do, and my baby mother is struggling like you are, and you have my daughter. So, I wanna be better for you and her. From here on out y'all are going to ball just as hard as I do. And I'm going to start treating you better. That's my word, well, I mean after tonight."

Fancy was with him until the last part. "Wait what do you mean about after tonight?"

Javier smoked the blunt until it was halfway gone, then he stubbed it out on a small plate that was on the table. "Tonight, I'm finna take that pussy for old time's sake." He pulled his shirt over his head and stood before her in a beater and a bulletproof vest.

Fancy backed away from him and dropped the bat. "Javier don't play with me. Sex is the furthest thing from my mind."

Javier shrugged his shoulders. Sudan's sexy chocolate body crossed his mind, he became aroused. He imagined sliding into Fancy and trembled. "Fancy bring yo' ass here." He stepped forward and took hold of her.

Fancy pushed him back, but it did little to move him in the slightest. "Get away from me, Javier, I'm not in the mood." She thought about breaking away from him and picking up the bat.

Javier pulled her down to the floor and ripped her robe apart. He yanked her panties off with one tug and moved her thighs out of the way so that he could position himself between her thighs. He pulled his dick out and rubbed her pussy. "I don't give a fuck who you mess with when I ain't here but whenever I want some of this pussy, and I'm here I'm taking this shit. It's as simple as that." He pulled her further to him and slipped his piece right on her entrance.

Fancy slapped at him, he leaned his body weight on her and thrust forward impaling himself deep into her womb. Her hotness enveloped him. He groaned and stayed as deep as he could. His mind flashed back to Sudan, and the dark color of her skin. He imagined Sudan once again in the tight white skirt. He shivered and began to stroke Fancy at full speed holding onto her shoulders while she moaned for him to get off her.

Fancy dug her nails into his shoulders and scratched as fiercely as she could. "Get off me, Javier! Please, get off me! Uhhhh!"

Javier was deep inside of Sudan even though it was Fancy underneath him. He closed his eyes tighter and fucked her like an animal on the Den's floor. She clawed at his back and bit into his neck in a mock attempt to get him off her, but it only added to his level of pleasure. "Uh! Uh! Uh! Talk that shit now, Sudan! Uh! Uh!" His back rolled and slammed forward.

He took out all his anger between Fancy's thighs plunging so deep into her that her screams of protest became those of pleasurable moans. She humped into him and gasped with her mouth wide open. She rubbed all over his back and wrapped her slim ankles around his waist. Javier continued to fuck her royally. His dick plunged in and out of her hot womb like a battering ram. When it came time for him to cum, he pulled out and came all over her neck and face, jerking his piece over and over until he was done.

Chapter 12

Cecelia slid her arm around Joaquin's waist and laid her head on his shoulder. It was her twenty-third birthday, and he had promised to take her out on the tourist section of the island where he was sure she would have a ball. Cecelia was dressed for the occasion in a brand-new dark red Nine West dress that Joaquin had gotten for her. She felt pretty and couldn't wait to be seen with Joaquin. His name was buzzing around La Perla, and he'd already paid all their household bills and bought them a new car to get around the island. Cecelia didn't know what Joaquin had come up on, but she was thirsty to be a part of the action. She wanted all the women in La Perla to know he was with her. She was even willing to fight over him. To be seen as his woman meant that much to her.

Joaquin was feeling guilty, tonight was the night that both he and Emilia were going to let it be known that they loved and wanted to be with each other. Joaquin honestly felt a deep affection for Cecilia, but he didn't love her as much as he loved Emilia. The thought of Emilia leaving the island and going away to New York City to live her life with Franco was enough to help Joaquin realize how much he really loved and adored her. He couldn't fathom life without Emilia, and to-night was the night that he was to let it be known.

Emilia came down the steps with her hand inside of Franco's. She wore a tight-fitting blue and orange dress that accentuated her curves and brought attention to her slim yet thick figure. She avoided Joaquin's eye contact, though she could tell he was staring at her for two reasons. The first was because she was killing her dress, and the second was because she was still holding Franco's hand.

"Damn, Emilia, it's supposed to be my birthday and you're killing it. Ooo-we, Franco, I already know where things are headed tonight." Cecilia teased and snuggled more firmly under Joaquin. "Doesn't she look good, Joaquin?" She looked up at him.

"Yeah, she does," he said this faintly. His eyes were pinned on her hand being connected with Franco's. Joaquin could feel himself getting angry.

"Yeah, she's killing it, though, lucky Franco. But it's all good, Joaquin, you got me, and—" She pulled him down so she could whisper in his ear. "Tonight, for my birthday I'm going to let you fuck me in any hole you want. We're going all out, as long as you give me my liquid courage," she spoke in terms of alcohol and lots of it.

That was one of the few things Joaquin didn't like about Cecilia. It was the fact that she liked to drink daily, and when she went out to clubs, she liked to get pissy drunk. He found that unattractive, and the sex that usually followed was never appealing to him. He didn't really like females with excessive user habits. Occasional drinking or smoking was cool, but all the time was gross to him. He also didn't like the fact that Cecilia smoked cigarettes. These were a few things that left his eyes wandering.

"So, what are we about to do? Are we going to have a good time or what?" Cecilia was already tipsy and ready to party.

Franco placed his arm possessively around Emilia's shoulders. "Let's have the time of our lives because I might not be back to the island for a while once Emilia and I are married. We're looking to have a bunch of rug rats running around the house right away. Hell, we may already be ahead of the curb." He placed his hand over Emilia's stomach.

Emilia moved his hand. "Franco shut up, and don't ruin the evening. Now let's go so we can have a good time with Cecilia tonight." She walked to the Joaquin's new Cadillac

Escalade and opened the door before she climbed into the back of it.

Franco and Cecilia followed close behind them. They disappeared into the truck while Joaquin stood frozen outside. "Pregnant?" he whispered to himself. "Emilia might be pregnant by this clown?" He mugged Franco through the glass of the truck. They locked eyes, then Franco looked off into the other direction.

He wanted to find out right then and there if Emilia was pregnant, but he also didn't want to cause a stir or ruin Cecilia's night. Both he and Emilia had already agreed that they would wait until midnight before they expressed their true feelings for each other to Franco and Cecilia.

"Baby, what are you waiting on? Let's go, you already know that the club is going to be packed." Cecilia called rolling down the window.

Joaquin snapped out of his zone and placed a fake smile on his face. "Yeah, a'ight here I come."

***

It was a quarter to midnight and three hours later when Cecilia slid her arms around Joaquin's neck and rested her head on his chest. He held her waist and rocked her from side to side. Though he held her in his arms his attention was across the dance floor where he gazed into Emilia's pretty eyes. She gazed back at him longing for the best friend that she had always loved and known her entire life. Franco held Emilia tighter and relished in the feel of her soft body against his. He dared to kiss her cheek. She became uncomfortable.

Joaquin felt the beast coming out of him. The club was packed but no matter how packed it was he managed to maneuver Cecilia on the dance floor so he could keep an eye on

Emilia. When Franco moved his hand down and cuffed Emilia's ass, he thought he would lose his mind. Emilia removed Franco's hand, but it was too late the image had already been painted in his head. Joaquin stepped back and tried to gather himself, his muscles flexed. He saw images of Franco with his head blown off. He saw Franco hanging from a tree. He saw him kneeling on one knee cutting Franco up into little bitty pieces of Fish food, and the images seemed to calm his spirit.

"Baby, what's the matter? I can tell that somethin' is wrong. Should we sit down for a minute?" She was worried.

Joaquin took ahold of her hand. "Yeah, let's do that. Come on, let's go to our booth in the back of the club."

"Okay." Cecilia took his hand and allowed him to lead them back to their booth.

When they got there Joaquin cleaned off the couch for her and guided her so that she sat. He slid across from her and took a sip of his drink. "Damn." He didn't know where to begin.

"What's the matter, did I do something?" Cecilia reached out so she could touch his wrist. "Talk to me."

Joaquin held his back straight and took ahold of her hands. "Cecilia, you know that I am a very stand up and honest man. I do not like to beat around the bush, and I refuse to play games with anybody. The length of time that I already have makes me sick to my stomach."

"O-kay—" She was confused as to where he was going with things.

He exhaled again. "I didn't wanna do this on your birthday, but every day before this day I've seen how hard your mother's death has been on you. The last thing I want to do is to add to your discomfort but I gotta be real with you."

"Joaquin, what is going on? Talk to me."

Before Joaquin could say anything, Franco stepped up beside the table with a scowl on his face. "Is this true, you and Emilia?"

"Him and Emilia what?" Cecilia stood up, she looked down at Joaquin, then over at Emilia.

"Emilia tells me that her and this Cabròn want to be together. She says that they have been wanting to tell us this for weeks and haven't because of your need for healing with Martha's death."

"Is this true, Emilia, you and Joaquin?" Cecelia asked.

Emilia walked up to her sister slowly. "Cecilia, I never wanted to hurt you. Me and Joaquin have been in love since we were children. The only reason we have not acted on our love is because of the two of you, and we didn't want to ruin our friendship."

Cecilia stepped up to Emilia and smacked her as hard as she could. A nice bit of Emilia's lipstick was now on Cecilia's fingers. "You only want him now because he has come into some kind of money, and because of how those on the island revere him. You were so quick to kick him to the curb for Franco when you thought Joaquin was going to be a bum forever. Now you want to live a good life through him. You're such a hypocrite." She spit at her feet and wiped her mouth. "And you Joaquin, do you want her over me, huh?" She walked up on him.

Joaquin stood up and adjusted the two .40 Glocks in his waist. "Cecilia, maybe this isn't the best place to discuss all of this."

"That's not a fuckin' answer. Do you want my little sister over me? Answer the fucking question right now or so help me God."

"I love Emilia. I have been in love with her ever since we were kids, I just never knew it." Joaquin gazed into Emilia's eyes.

"You son of a bitch, you weren't thinking about Emilia until I wanted to marry her. Now all the sudden you're head over heels. I should—"

Joaquin came around the table. "Muthafucka you should know Cabròn?" Joaquin was done allowing Franco to call him out of his name or to get away with acting like he wanted to cause him bodily harm.

Franco balled up his fists. "I never liked you. From the first day that Emilia introduced us, I could see the utter disdain in your eyes. I knew you were going to be trouble. But you know what I am willing to fight you to death over her. If you whoop my ass I'll back off, but if I whoop yours then she is mine."

The night club continued to press forward behind them. People were dancing and grinding on each other having a great time.

Emilia pulled Franco by the arm and turned him so that he was facing her. "Who do you think you are? This is twenty fucking twenty, not the old caveman days. I don't give a shit if you whoop Joaquin or not, I am in love with him and he is who I am going to be with. It's over!" She pushed him out of her face.

Franco raised his hand to smack the shit out of her as Cecilia had. Joaquin swung and punched him so hard that he did a one-eighty and fell to the ground knocked out cold. The crowd jumped back. Joaquin pulled him up by his shirt. He took his Glock out of his belt and stuffed it into Franco's mouth. "If you ever think about laying a finger on Emilia again, I will kill you in cold blood with no hesitation. Now she is done with you. Get yo shit and get the fuck off the island of

Puerto Rico, or else." He cocked the hammer and stuffed it so far down Franco's throat that he gagged and threw up over the gun. Joaquin wanted to slay him.

Emilia placed her hand on his wrist. "It's okay, Joaquin, give him a past. He will leave. Our secret is out there now."

Cecilia grabbed Joaquin's wrist and pulled him out of the club. She kept pulling him until they were ways into the parking lot. Then she stopped and looked up at him with tears in her eyes. "I will never forgive you for as long as I live. You broke my heart. I thought you were the one." She wiped her tears away. "What makes it even worse is that it's for my own little sister. I feel so useless." She slapped him.

Joaquin took the lick and tasted the blood in his mouth. "I'm sorry."

She shook her head. "No, not right now. But one day you will be." She pushed him away from her and walked off.

As she disappeared Emilia came up and took his hand. "Seems like it's just you and me now, Joaquin. She's going to disown me. I will have no place to live."

"So, we will live together. I have wanted to live with you all my life. Now is the time." Then a thought clicked in his brain. "Wait a minute. Are you preg—"

"No, and don't even say it. Come on, we need to make it back to my home before she burns all my things." She pulled him along with a smile and a feeling weight having been lifted off her shoulders.

Chapter 13

It had been three days since Joaquin and Emilia had confessed their love for one another, and while Emilia had expected Cecilia to have been angry at her for a short time, she never expected her sister to completely treat her as if she no longer existed. On the first night after the revelation, Cecilia stopped Emilia as she was getting a few things out of her room so she could leave with Joaquin, Cecilia had stopped her and told her that they were no longer sisters from that point on and that she cursed the day that, Martha their mother, ever bought Emilia home from the hospital. The words were enough to shatter Emilia's soul and to break her fragile heart that she possessed for her sister down the middle. So much so that it had been three days, and she had yet to get out of the bed for anything more than using the bathroom and eating a meal.

On the third night after the revelation, Joaquin came home to find her still wrapped up in the sheets. He had stopped at Juanitos and picked them up dinner for the night. He took the bag of food, set it on the dresser of the room, and skidded into the bed next to Emilia. He pulled her up so that she was resting with her head on his chest.

He wrapped his right arm around her. "You know Emilia sooner or later you're going to have to get over the harsh things Cecilia said to you out of her anger. She didn't mean them, and it didn't help that she got the news about us on her birthday. Time will pass, and she will become better. Trust me on this."

"Cecilia was the only best friend that I had. She understood me. I feel so alone, right now." She rolled over and placed her back to him.

Joaquin rubbed it. "Damn, Emilia, I'm telling you that things will get better, you have to trust."

"Joaquin, how do you know, huh?" She sat up and faced him. "We hurt two people at one time. Two people that swore up and down that they were in love with us. How could we do such a thing?" She scooted out of the bed and stood up. Her long hair was wild and all over the place. The long white tee shirt she wore was wrinkled and had two juice stains on it.

Joaquin stepped up to her and took her hands. "Emilia, we knew this was going to happen. Now that it has, you're freaking out. I think you need to calm down."

She yanked her hands away from him. "Don't tell me to calm down, Joaquin. You didn't lose a whole sister like I did. In fact, you didn't lose anything in order for our relationship to come into existence. I lost my sister and another family that was willing to accept me as their daughter. They were my ticket off the island the married way, but I gave it up because of you. I just hate myself because I've always been in love with you and your ugly face." She turned her back to him again and crossed her arms in front of her.

Joaquin smiled and slowly crept behind her. He pulled her into his embrace. "I'm in love with you, Emilia. You were made for me. I have known this ever since the day you threw up on me when we were three years old." He kissed the back of her neck. "I'm going to work to make sure that I give you everything you need and want. I know what you desire, and I understand what you stood to gain by marrying Franco. I see what he had to offer; I promise to give just as much if not more. All you have to do is to give me a chance. Can you do that?"

"So, now you think I am like the average girl here in La Perla. You think that all it boils down to me for me is a series of gifts and things you can buy? Really, that's how you feel?"

"I'm not saying that."

"Then what are you saying, Joaquin?"

"I'm saying that I intend to give you the greatest life I possibly can as your man. I want to make you happy. I want to spoil you."

"Franco wanted to marry me. He saw me as his wife. How do you see me?" She turned around in his embrace so she could look into his eyes. "Please tell me, I need to hear it."

Joaquin placed his big hands on the sides of her small face and gazed into her eyes. "When I was little my mother often read the story of Genesis from the Bible to me. In the story of Genesis, there was a man named Adam, and a woman named Eve. God was tired of Adam being alone. He'd laid the world before his feet, and yet Adam still felt incomplete and alone. Until God laid him down one day and took one of his ribs which are the strongest and most important structure inside the human body. He took the rib out of Adam and created for him his best half, Eve. When I look at you Emilia, I see my Eve. I see my best half and a creation that was made from me, for me. You are more than a wife. You are my reason. I love you, and I am going to marry you and give you a wedding better than one that Franco could ever think of."

Emilia felt herself becoming emotional. "How will you know what kind of wedding will make me happy? Have you ever asked me?" Her eyes become glossy.

"No, baby, I haven't. I'm asking you now. How can I make you the happiest woman in existence? What kind of wedding do you desire?" He rubbed the sides of her hair and helped her place some of the curly tufts behind her ears.

"I don't know now that Cecilia won't be there. Martha is already gone. Who else do I have that will even care about my special day? Nobody that's who." She grew depressed.

Joaquin rubbed her face with his thumbs. "My mother, Martina, would love to see you in your wedding dress. So would Justina, and so many other females from La Perla, and even San Juan. You are very well-liked. Besides all those people I would love to see you in a wedding dress. There is not a more beautiful girl in the world than you." He looked into her eyes. "Emilia, you are perfect, and nothing matters more to me in this world than you do."

Tears fell from her eyes. "Cecilia was the only real family I had left. She looked so much like my mother that at times I would pretend she was her. Whenever I did, I felt a sense of peace. I feel like my heart is broken, Joaquin. To lose a mother and a sister so close together is devastating. I don't know how strong I really am. It's killing me." She broke into a full fit of tears and grew weak against him.

Joaquin held her against his body and hugged her. "I understand, Emilia. I am here for you for as long as you need me to be. You are my baby, and I love you. Anything you need from me please just tell me."

Emilia cried harder. "I don't know what I need, Joaquin. I just know that I don't want to lose my sister. If only for a little while that I can deal with, but for eternity would kill me. I can't do it. Maybe you can go and talk to her for me. Tell her that I am sorry. I love her, and I never meant to hurt her. Tell her that although you and I are together it will never take away from how great of a sister I will be to her." She grabbed a handful of Joaquin's clothes. "Tell her that we just lost our mother, and I can't lose her too. That it would make me physically sick, and already it's driving me insane."

Joaquin held her tight. He didn't like feeling, or even knowing that Emilia was hurting. "I will go to her for you, Emilia. I will get her to have a change of heart. But please calm down. Please stop crying, I am begging you."

***

Cecilia came out of the kitchen with a hot plate of sausages and eggs. She set them on the table in front of Franco, along with a glass of Orange juice. "Here you go, Franco. I'll still never understand why you like breakfast food in the evening so much, but who am I to judge you?"

Franco pushed his laptop to the side of the table and looked over the food that Cecilia had set before him. "Wow it looks good, thank you."

"You're welcome, Franco." She went into the kitchen and grabbed her plate of food. She came back and sat across from him. "You're ready to go back to New York? I bet you can't wait to get the hell away from this place of pain, huh?" She tore into her sausages.

Franco stared at his food for a moment, and an image of Emilia came across his mind. He sighed in defeat. He looked across the table at Cecilia. Her long hair was extra curly in the morning because she was fresh out of the shower. The hair popped full of sheen. "I think I'm gonna miss you, Cecilia. I hate that while I was here, I didn't take more time to get to know you. You really are an amazing woman, and any man would be blessed to have such a diamond, I mean that."

Cecilia was caught off guard by his comments. She ran her fingers through her hair. "What made you say that, Franco?"

He shrugged his shoulders. "I just felt like it was appropriate. I'm starting to feel like all those summers I spent chasing behind Emilia should've been spent chasing you. I've always thought you were more beautiful, but so much so that you were out of my league. I hate myself for settling."

Cecilia dropped her fork. "So, what are you saying? Because your words are really screwing me up, right now? I am very vulnerable, and I feel so lost."

Franco pushed his plate away from him. "I'm saying why should we let them fuck us over like this. You're a flawlessly gorgeous woman. You're loyal, Puerto Rican, and full of zest. I have always secretly been enamored by you. Why shouldn't we see if we have anything in common? I'll bet you we do." He stood up.

Cecilia pushed her chair back from the table and stood up. "Franco, I swear to you that all I desire is an honest man that is willing to provide a stable home. I am an old-fashioned girl. I do not require much. If you are thinking what you are thinking, I am with it. The question is, what are you thinking?"

Franco came around the table and pulled Cecilia to him so hard that she yelped. He gripped her ass over the cotton sundress that she wore and rubbed all over it. "I've always wanted to do this." He pulled it up from the back until his hands met hot skin. He clutched her cheeks and kissed her neck. "Do you want me?"

Cecilia felt his dick become hard. She thought about Emilia and it gave her the driving force to push further. She stepped into his hard-on and allowed it to poke through her middle. "I want you, Franco! I want you so bad."

Franco picked her up and set her on the table. He pulled her panties down her hips and off her feet. Cecilia helped him get his dick out of his pants. As soon as it was free, she opened her thighs wider for him. Franco's dick head slid through her pussy lips and sunk deep into her body. They gasped into each other's faces. Cecilia was the first to open her eyes. She looked in Franco's face and knew that she was betraying her sister, and the act gave her heart tranquility. She locked her ankles around Franco's waist.

"Fuck me, Franco. Fuck me harder than you ever fucked my sister." Cecilia licked his neck and sucked on it.

Franco began to fuck her. He couldn't believe his luck. He'd been able to screw both sisters, he felt like that was every man's dream. It was most definitely his. He began to stroke her while holding onto her ass. She leaned backward to give him a better angle. "Uh! Uh! Uh, Cecilia! I knew it, I knew it would be better," he groaned.

Cecilia closed her eyes tight and imagined Joaquin having Emilia in the same position. She didn't understand why it aroused her, but it did. She scooted forward and humped into him faster and faster. She wanted his seed. If she could get him to cum in her a few times before he went back to New York she was sure, she would become pregnant, and if she could become pregnant, she could lock him down. He came from money, and money for Cecilia now that things had ended between her and Joaquin was most definitely the motive.

She sucked his neck. "Fuck this pussy harder. It's yours, come and get it."

Franco groaned and stroked. "Aw shit, Cecilia. Fuck!" He stood on his tippy toes and pounded as hard as he could. Her box got to feeling better and better to him. She was working her inner muscles and it became too much. Franco began to shake. He leaned forward cumming hard into Cecilia.

"Yes, Franco! Yes!" Cecilia felt his squirts and lowered her eyes while plotting. If she'd lost Joaquin, she would work to gain Franco, either way, she was done with being a loser. Money was the motive.

***

Joaquin helped Emilia come back to the ground after hoisting her up into her mother's living room shack window. He wanted her to see everything with her own eyes. Now that she had he wondered how it would affect her? Emilia got down and went around to the back of the shack. She opened the door and went inside. Cecilia had Franco on the floor riding him with her head thrown back in complete ecstasy. The shack smelled of heavy sex.

"I hope you two have a nice life together." She was calm. "Cecilia, I love you, and when you are ready to be sisters again contact me."

Cecilia ignored her. She placed both of her hands-on Franco's chest and rode him hard. His piece pounded in and out of her. Her cream seeped down his shaft and wet his balls underneath. Cecilia screamed and came watching Emilia as she walked away.

She felt vindicated by her actions. She laughed and kept riding him, bouncing down harder taking him deeper into her lower belly as much as she could.

Joaquin shook his head. "Y'all deserve each other." He scoffed. "I got Emilia for life." He meant it.

Chapter 14

Javier was tired of feeling like his efforts to be an heir to his father's throne was going unnoticed by Rodolfo, so he decided to turn things up a notch. He took the hundred-kilo shipment of coke that was imported from Columbia by private jet. Instead of sitting on it for the usual two weeks that Rodolfo usually recommended, Javier took it upon himself to flood the streets of Miami in a major way. Then he took five hundred thousand dollars of Rodolfo's money that Rodolfo kept hidden away in a safe for rainy days and purchased a hefty supply of tar Heroin from a connection that ran with the Sinaloa Cartel.

Once again instead of sitting on the new supply, he flooded the streets of Miami and even the southern part of Atlanta Georgia. Javier was on a mission for a month straight. Whenever their profits came to the sum of five hundred thousand, he copped more narcotics and flooded the streets without ceasing. In two months, the family business was thriving like never before and he and Rodolfo were making money hand over fist. Javier felt good, he felt responsible, and finally, he felt like he was earning his keep as the heir to the Peralta throne.

It was a Friday night when Javier and ten of his closest dope boy hustlers got fresh and loaded up into his Hummer limousine to celebrate the newfound success of the Peraltas. Javier had found two new plugs directly out of Mexico, and they were selling him quality products for dirt cheap. Off each kilo, he was making a six hundred percent profit. The numbers were crazy, and it allowed him to slowly move his business into Georgia where the demand for topnotch dope was high, but the quality supply was really low. Javier wanted to celebrate. He'd worked a month straight with no break, he felt like it was time.

When they pulled up to a five-star rated nightclub by the name of The Wall, Javier stepped out of the Hummer on the warm summer night dressed in a black and orange Yves St. Laurent fit, over the matching Balenciaga's. He had two million dollars-worth of rented gold jewelry hanging from his neck, and diamond studs in each ear that sparkled every time he turned his head. His nails were manicured, and on his left wrist was a dripping Patek watch that had so many yellow diamonds in it that it looked like he'd stuck his hand in a lemon snow cone and the product became glued to his wrist. He was fresh and smelling even better. His crew was more of the same.

He pushed the Chanel gold frames back on the bridge of his nose, as he stepped up to the bodyguard that stood in front of the entrance to the club. "The name is Javier Peralta." There was a long line of people waiting to get into the hot new club.

The bodyguard scrolled down his iPad and found his name. "I found you. You're good to go, but this only says a party of four. It looks like you got way more than that with you, bruh. You gotta send some home," he advised.

Javier pulled a two thousand dollar knot out of his pocket that he had in all fifties. He slipped it to the security man. "Now tell me what that screen says."

The security guard tucked the cash and pulled back the velvet ropes. "It says have a good night."

Javier nodded. "That's what the fuck I thought, Papi." He waved for his crew to follow him inside where they were waved over with a metal-detecting wand. Then they were actually made to walk through a metal detector.

After all that chaos Javier and his crew were led through a jammed pack crowd of dancing patrons. Women were

114

twerking on the men or women that they had come with. Some women were dancing with drinks in their hands, and a bunch of dudes were doing the same thing. As Javier and his crew walked through the crowd there were a bunch of women that pulled at his wrist or tried to get him to stop so they could talk to him. He ignored them having not seen any that caught his fancy.

When they made it to the VIP section he slid into the couch and ordered ten bottles of Ace of Spade and two gallons of Patron. He sat back like a boss and placed his cellphone on his lap. Two of his dope boys stood behind the couch on security while the eight others were ready to enjoy the night out. Javier had already told them that he planned for them to go another month straight hustlin' without many breaks in between. He meant that.

"Fellas," he began holding a bottle of Ace of Spades in one hand, and a glass of Patron in the other. "The ten of you that are with me tonight are the ones I have chosen to get on this rich nigga shit with me. All your hard work and loyalty is going to pay off real soon. Tonight, I just wanted to show you a token of my appreciation." He took a sip from the bottle of Champagne, then stood up and gave a head nod to the owner of the club.

Thirty seconds later ten of the baddest dancers in Miami made their way into the V.I.P. section where Javier's men were. The ladies were dressed in short designer skirts and high heels. They were thick and flawlessly gorgeous. The V.I.P. section filled up with the scent of lady perfume almost immediately. The girls chose the man that they liked the most and sat next to him to get to know them in a more familiar way. Javier's ken didn't waste any time running their hands over the women's thighs and squeezing them. Javier nodded his approval and laughed. The feeling of being a boss was starting to overcome him.

Federal Agent Finesse Jenkins stood five-feet-three inches tall, dark-skinned, with natural brown eyes, and a short hairstyle that fit her to the tee. She had the body of a topnotch model grossing stripper, and she knew she was bad. She stepped into Javier's V.I.P. section with her lips glossed, and her Fendi outfit hugging her like a second skin. She eyed him from across the small expanse of the section.

Javier saw her skin complexion and immediately began to feel some type of way. He stood up and slipped through the other females that were present to extend his hand to Finesse. The Patek watch sparkled under the night club's lights. "Mamita, please tell me you came in last because you were waiting to spend some time with the boss. What is your name?"

Finesse looked him up and down while she shook his head. "I've been in Miami only for a short time, but I know a boss when I see one. This display you're putting on doesn't amuse me. I've seen it done better by true bosses. My name is Finesse. What is your name again?" She knew flexing on Javier was the easiest way to pick into the lock that was him. She was familiar with his ego. The unit had recorded him enough to profile him. Finesse wanted to attack his ego before she conquered him.

Javier laughed. "My name is Javier Peralta. I am the son of Rodolfo Peralta. I got the streets of Miami, and soon I will have those of Atlanta as well."

"Well, you'll have to excuse me because I have no idea what you mean. This is only my first month in Miami. I am here from Chicago, Illinois. My sorority sister, that Puerto Rican girl right there invited me out with her tonight. The owner of the club told us he would pay us a hefty sum to spend some quality time with you boys. I turned him down, but obviously, Reeka did not. So, I'm just watching out for her until she earns her money, then we're out of here."

"Oh, no, now that I have seen that Miami can hold something this fine, and this flawless. There is no way I am about to let you act as a chaperon without me getting to know you."

"Oh, is that so?"

"Yeah, that's so." He took another sip from his champagne.

"And will you be playing this tired Boss role the entire time? Or will it be smart of me to cut off your word supply, right now?" She rolled her eyes and crossed her arms in front of her.

"It's not an act. These are my men. I run to them, and they answer me. Miami is my city. It's where I eat, and it's where I am getting rich as a bitch. Now I don't know you, but this whole jazzy thing is working in your favor. How much is your time worth to you?" He fanned his hand through the air and guided her toward his vacant seat on the V.I.P. section's couch.

"Very valuable, and n'all this flashy shit isn't my thing. I'm more of a solo girl. If you want to get to know me, and what I'm all about, you'd leave with me right now. We could go and have a quiet dinner at McCoy's a short way down the strip."

"What about, Reeka? I thought you were her protector?" He looked over his shoulder at Reeka. She was sitting on one of his dope boy's laps and giving him a lap dance while she held onto his neck. She whispered whore like things into his ear and laughed at her own brazenness. Reeka was trying to check a bag.

Finesse waved Reeka off. "There are cameras there, and there." She pointed them out for him to see. "As long as you give your men the order to not leave this section there is nothing I will have to worry about. She was paid to entertain them, so as long as they are here, she will be also." Finesse knew Reeka was actually undercover and her real name was Marcia Salazar.

"In order for a man to make a bunch of other grown men stay in one place while he frolics with a woman the one giving the order must be a boss, which brings me back to my first point."

Finesse rolled her eyes again. "Oh, my God! Are we going to go and chill or what? You're boring me already." She looked past his shoulder to Reeka?

Reeka looked up at her and gave her a look that said she was okay, and she had everything under control back there.

Javier nodded. "You see all these diamonds, and all this drip and you're still talking crazy. Yeah, I gotta see what you're all about. Let me give the word to my homies and let them know, I will be back in a few hours. Then me and you can roll out." He spun away from her and did exactly that.

***

"So, tell me, Javier. What made you get into the dope game?" Finesse picked at her Chicken Salad. It was her favorite dish at McCoy's, but she found it so hard to focus on the meal at the juncture. She couldn't believe it had been so easy to pull Javier away from The Wall. Not only did he leave behind his crew, but he'd stepped away from all them and hadn't arranged for security to come with him. He was an idiot is what Finesse thought. Had she been a jacker, or somebody that was trying to set him up to be robbed or killed she would have been successful.

Javier rubbed his hands together and smiled at her. "My pops is a Drug Lord and I'm his heir. I was born to be a boss. I didn't choose this life; it chose me at birth." He took his fork and stabbed a piece of chicken from her plate and ate it.

Finesse frowned at him. "Excuse you, do you think we are that cool?" She pushed her salad away from her.

"I think you have some of the sexiest skin I have ever seen in my life. Not only that but you were the finest woman in The Wall, and you're the finest woman here as well. I'm astonished."

Finesse was caught off guard. "Thank you, but that still doesn't give you the right to stab your lil' nasty fork into my salad. Next time you need to ask me if you can invade my property like that."

Javier went into his pocket and laid a hundred-dollar bill on the plate. "The salad is on me. I do apologize, I won't allow it to happen again. But I meant what I said about your beauty."

"And I said thank you. What else were you expecting?"

Before Javier could respond two men ran into the restaurant with assault rifles in their hands. They were armed with bulletproof vests, and bodysuits to protect them from slugs fired by guns. They were on a bloody mission unbeknownst to the patrons at McCoy's

"Everybody get the fuck down unless you want to die!" the head gunmen hollered from under his mask.

"There is no talking necessary! Do away with the injustices that are aimed at enslaving the brown community!" He began firing shot after shot with the intention of killing everyone present that wasn't his crime partner.

Chapter 15

Javier jumped from his seat and pulled Finesse down to the floor of the restaurant. The other patrons were in a frenzy. They screamed and fell to the floor. The ones that jumped up immediately became targets by the gunmen. Both shooters locked into the vulnerable victims. They sprayed their assault rifles with deadly intent.

Boom! Boom! Boom! Boom!

Finesse curled into a ball and pulled her wire as close to her face as possible. "I am okay," she whispered. "I repeat, I am okay, do not blow my cover." She kept her back to Javier and decided to play the woman in a distressed role; the gunmen continued to pick off one patron after the next.

Javier climbed atop of her. "Be cool, Mami, I got you. I ain't gon' let these mafuckas kill you, I promise." Javier had been selfish his whole life.

All he'd ever cared about was himself, but there was something special about Finesse that made him want to save her. There was something about her that made him feel the need for her. He held her tight and peeked to see where the shooters were. Two more people that were trying to run out of the front door of the restaurant were slain. They fell to the ground and began to shake until their life drifted away from them. The shooters started to move toward the front of the restaurant. Javier looked toward the back and saw a big exit sign.

"Finesse you've been to this club before, right?" The other patrons were whimpering and crying. The faint scent of feces emanated into the air.

"Yeah, like four other times. Why?" Finesse whispered.

"Because I need to know if there is an exit outback. If so, do you think we can make it to it before the gunmen get to us?"

Finesse wanted to tell him that she had a small .9 millimeter in her Hermes bag. She wanted to jump up and go into action. She was a decorated Federal Agent. She saw how sloppily the two shooters carried on. She would have no problem scoping and killing them with lethal headshots. Instead of exposing her hand, she convinced herself that getting indictments for the Peralta case was more important. The bust was set to be large, it spanned across the United States, and ventured to the Islands. If she could bust Rodolfo Peralta by use of his son and inevitable heir to the Peralta throne, then she could move up the ladder in the Federal Agency and finally slide into a Pentagon seat.

She nodded her head at her own pondering. "Yeah, there is an exit outback. If we get up and break for it like crazy, we should be able to make it. Is that what you have in mind?"

Javier pulled her closer to him. "Hell yeah, and I'm strapped. Come on, I wanna get you up out of here." He pulled a .40 Glock from his belt and cocked it.

He slowly eased off Finesse and peeked down the expanse of the restaurant. He saw the shooters walking from table to table gunning down the people that were ignorant enough to hide under them.

"Well, if we're going to do this, you're going to have to protect me. Don't let those bad guys get to me, Javier. Please, I'm so scared." She made herself shake.

"You got my word that ain't shit like that about to happen. Come on, on the count of three you're going to take off running and I'm going to cover you. Are you ready?"

"Yeah, as ready as I will get." She came to her knees and looked down the row of tables. The scent of burnt flesh and gunpowder was heavy in the air. "Shit, it looks like they're coming back this way." She saw the gunmen slowly making their way toward the back of the restaurant. She began to become nervous.

"A'ight, it's time to go then." He was on one knee. "On the count of three. One, two, three. Go!"

"Okay!" Finesse jumped up and took off running.

As soon as the gunmen saw her headed for the back of the restaurant they paused and got ready to raise their firearms. Javier jumped up and began bucking in their direction. *Blocka! Blocka! Blocka! Blocka!* Bullets zipped from his gun and slammed into both shooters. They fell backward and landed on tables. Patrons jumped up and headed for the exits. Javier kept shooting. He tried to give them dome shots, but his aim sucked. He only wound up hitting up their body armor again sending them ducking for cover. As they were ducking for cover, he took off running behind Finesse. In seconds they were in her car. She threw open the door for Javier, and he jumped inside. Then she pulled away from the scene knowing that the Agency was going to debrief her about it as soon as they could.

***

"Peto, why are you staring at me like that? You're making me feel so uncomfortable, right now." Kelis bounced Alexis up and down on her hip. She hadn't been around Peto in a week, and neither had Alexis. Peto had hit her up on Facebook telling her that he missed her and the baby. He begged her to come to his mother's house where he could see them, and Kelis had relented. When she arrived, she found out that Tracy was nowhere in sight, it was just Peto.

"I've been with you since you were sixteen years old, and we have a daughter together. Now you're saying that I am making you uncomfortable?" Peto held out his hands so that she could hand him, Alexis.

Kelis handed him their daughter. "I just don't like it when anybody looks at me without saying a word. I would prefer for you to speak, that's all I'm saying. The last time we were together things didn't end so well. I'm still kind of dwelling on that."

Peto held Alexis in his arms and looked her over. Though she was a baby her features were strongly Kelis'. He saw very little trace of himself in her. "I think that you have fallen out of love with me and that you crave Javier now. There is no way for me to compete with a man that has everything. I can only supply you with the basics, and clearly, that is not enough for you." He sat on the couch with Alexis.

"When will you understand that things mean nothing to me? My God, Peto, if you provided the basics that would be more than enough for me and Alexis. The thing with you is that you can't even provide the basics. You'd rather spend your money on drugs and alcohol like a loser and allow me and your daughter to suffer."

Peto picked up Alexis and bounced her up and down on his knee. She smiled at him, deep dimples popped on her cheeks. Flashes of Javier's dimples came into his mind. He began to really look the baby over. "So, is that what you think I am, some loser?"

"I'm not saying that I said it's how you act at times. I just don't understand why it's so hard for you to get it together." She took a deep breath and tried to center herself.

"Now that I look at Alexis, I need to ask you a serious question." He sat Alexis down, turned the baby's back to him and rested her up against his chest.

"What is the question, Peto?" She sat across from him.

"Is Alexis even my daughter or does she belong to Javier?"

124

"Javier!" She jumped up. "That's it! Give me my baby. Now, Peto!"

Peto stood up with Alexis. "Calm down it's only a question. A yes or no answer will suffice. Is she his?"

"Give me my daughter, Peto!"

"Waaahhh!" Alexis began to cry and scream.

Peto turned his back to Kelis and held the baby tighter. "No! This is my baby, too. She belongs to me just as much as she belongs to you. Unless she is Javier's. If that's the case then you can have her, and I don't want anything to do with you for the rest of my life. Now is she mine?"

Kelis thought about it long and hard. There was a one hundred percent chance that Alexis was Peto's daughter because she'd gotten pregnant the first time, they'd had sex, and prior to Javier, Peto had been the only man that she'd ever slept with. But she looked at the way Peto was holding Alexis so dangerously. The baby looked as if she were about to slip from his arms. She figured that if she told him that Alexis wasn't his child, he would release her to her. She could always tell him the truth later.

"You're right. I'm sorry, she is Javier's. I wanted to tell you."

Peto felt like the world was crashing down around him. His heart dropped into his stomach. He looked down at Alexis and two tears dropped from the corners of his eyes. Suddenly he snapped. He held Alexis as high into the air as he could.

"I hate you, Kelis. I hate you so much!" He slammed Alexis to the floor and threw the glass table as hard as he could. She ricocheted off the floor and laid screaming her little heart out. Shards of glass were stuck into her precious skin.

"Noooo!" Kelis wailed. She ran to pick Alexis up from the floor.

Peto was out of his mind. He grabbed her by the hair and yanked her head backward. "You selfish, bitch! My baby ain't even mine!" He flung her to the ground.

Kelis was a mother bear in protection of her cub. She bounced up from the carpet with her eyes lowered. Peto was no longer Peto to her. He was now the man that had assaulted her defenseless child. She ran at him with her nails bared. She gouged at his face and took a sufficient amount of skin off it. She headbutted him so hard that she busted his nose, then she jumped on top of him swinging like a mad woman which she was at that moment. She bit a plug out of his cheek.

Peto hollered and fell against the wall. He bounced off it with his face dripping blood. "Bitch, I'm finna kill you."

Kelis attacked again; she punched wildly hitting his face, both eyes, and his forehead. She kneed him in the nuts and threw him to the floor. He curled into a ball groaning in absolute pain. She looked to her right and saw Alexis reaching out for her. She ran over and scooped up her baby. She pulled the shards of glass out of her one at a time doing more harm than good. Each shard that she pulled out caused a flow of blood to ensue.

Kelis burst into tears. "I gotta get my baby to a hospital. Please, Santa Maria!" she screamed.

She ran to the front door and was about to open it when she remembered that she didn't have her car keys. She hurried to the back of the house to grab them off the dresser. By the time she made it back to the hallway, Peto was blocking her path with a steak knife in one hand, and a butcher's knife in the other.

"Peto, please, Alexis is dying. Please don't let our baby die. I swear to the heavens that she is your daughter. I am sorry for lying to you," she cried walking closer.

Peto lowered his head. His nose was bleeding profusely. "You never loved me. Any bitch that can sleep with my cousin could never love me. But I loved you, Kelis. I loved you with all my heart and I woulda never hurt you intentionally. But now you have to die." He walked toward her with both knives.

Alexis stopped moving, the life had left her little body, and it was like Kelis knew it. She began to cry. She held her baby to her chest. "You're evil, Peto. You're an evil man and I forgive you. Me and my daughter forgive you. Now send me to Jesus with her! This world is full of too much pain and agony for me. I only want to be with Alexis." She kneeled down on her knees and held Alexis to her chest.

Peto was determined to have no mercy. He ran up and stabbed Kelis in the throat, pulled the blade out, and slammed it into her again. Then he fell on top of her stabbing over and over like a madman until life left her body. He lay there crying next to his girls, then he snapped again and began stabbing both of them over and over again until.

"I'm sorry—I'm so sorry," Peto wailed as tears streamed down his face to both Kelis and Alexis before fainting on top of Kelis.

Chapter 16

Three days after the massacre shooting at McCoy's, Finesse had been debriefed by the Agency, and so had Javier in an unrelated way. Even though she was placed on Javier's case to infiltrate Rodolfo's Narcotics Empire. Finesse as a woman had to appreciate how Javier had stood up for her and placed his life on the line so that she could get out of the restaurant with hers intact. Her goal of entering the Pentagon remained at the forefront of her mind, while at the same time she had to admit that she enjoyed his company.

On the third day after the shooting Javier invited Finesse for a date out on the waters. She graciously accepted it off the books, though she already knew she would find it hard to stay away from work while she and him were spending the quality time together. Once again she had to admit how he treated her as a lady.

Javier held out his hand and helped Finesse to climb into the seventy-five-foot rented Yacht. He knew it was rented, but when it came to flexing Javier was going to do all he could, to make sure Finesse didn't know that his boat was rented. It was a pride thing.

"Mamamita come on and bring yo' lil' sexy self on board so I can be blessed with that booty. I mean beauty." He laughed. He was rocking an all-white Ralph Lauren short set over sockless Polo slippers.

"Mmm-hmm, you better clean that up. I hope you don't think just because you threw your life on the line for me, I owe you something. This ain't no romance movie."

"If it were, you'd already be in love with me." He held her until she stepped onto the deck.

Finesse was wearing an all-white Burberry sundress that clung to her curves just right. Her perfume drifted over to him and made him feel a way. "I know dang 'ol well, Javier the Miami Playboy ain't using no sentence with the word love in it. I don't know who you think you are running game on but you have the wrong person." She smiled at him, and locked eyes. "Why don't you show me around this piece of crap." She was fronting big time, but she knew when it came to locking down a major baller in the game like Javier Peralta the more he stunted to make things seem as if they were first class, a girl had to crap on them to keep him honest and chasing her. Rich men hated to be ignored, and they hated even worse for their efforts to go unnoticed. That was gold-digging 101.

Javier felt like his ego was bruised. "Awe, so that's how you gon' do me? You gon' say that this is a piece of crap? Are you kidding me? It cost me ten gees for the Captain alone, and that's every four hours. This boat was a gift to me," he lied. "I need to find a steady person to navigate it for me though, but that's just rich people problems, huh?"

Finesse shrugged her shoulders. "I guess." The sun reflected off her dark skin. It made her look like an African bombshell. "So, what are we going to do? I mean you invited me out here and all that."

Javier kissed her hand. "I just wanted to spend some time with you damn. I'd think that after our near-death experience, we would have a few things in common. If nothin' else just the night that we shared together. Do that mean anything to you?"

Finesse could tell Javier was getting angry. She didn't want to ruin the evening. It was essential that they got closer. She grabbed ahold of him and pulled him to her with aggression. Her lips caught his, and she kissed him as passionately as she could.

Javier took ahold of that chunky ass and cuffed it. She was so strapped, and it felt even better to him. He kissed her with more passion than he had ever shown any other female in his life. He really adored Finesse. When their lips parted, he stood back trying to catch his breath. His heart was pounding harder than it had ever pounded from a kiss. "Damn."

Finesse felt the connection. There were tingles all over her body. She felt moisture building between her thighs and she didn't like it. The feeling he gave her from one kiss was enough to let her know that playing around romantically with Javier was going to be both difficult and dangerous.

She wiped her kiss away with her thumb. "So, are you going to show me around the boat or what?"

It took a second for Javier to gather himself, but then he nodded his head. "Yeah, let me show you around."

***

"Psst! Psst! Fancy wake up," Peto whispered. He was standing over her bed while she slept with Vatican on the left side of her.

It was three days after he'd murdered both Kelis and Alexis. He'd spent all three days hugged with their corpses until the corpses began to swell and explode. The smelled so putrid that Peto was forced to get up and do something about it.

Vatican was the first to awake. She rubbed her eyes, and when they finally focused a bloody Peto came into view. She started screaming at the top of her lungs. "Mommy! Mommy! A monster! A monster! Help me! Wake up please!"

Fancy rolled out of bed and jumped up. She became light-headed from the sleep medication that she'd taken prior to her rest. She fell to one knee and was ready to throw up. Vatican continued to scream. Fancy got back up, she saw Peto with the dried blood all over his face, clothes and hair.

Her eyes got bucked. "What the fuck?"

Peto grabbed Vatican and placed his hand around her mouth. "Tell her little ass to shut up before the neighbors call the police," he growled. He smelled horrible, like death and feces.

Fancy smacked at his hands and pulled Vatican away from him. She picked her up. "Peto, what the hell are you doing in my house?" she hollered eyeing the blood all over him. Then Javier came to her mind. "Wait a minute. Did you do it? Is he—" She looked down at Vatican, and caught herself.

Peto ran his blood dried fingers through his hair. "I fucked up, Fancy. I need your help. I need your help so bad." He felt like he was on the verge of becoming hysterical.

Fancy carried Vatican out of the bedroom and to her bedroom. She kneeled down in front of her. "Baby listen to me. I need you to be a big girl for Mommy, okay?"

Vatican had seen the blood on Peto, it made her scared. She was thinking that he was a big, scary monster, and he was coming to get her as soon as Fancy wasn't looking. This terrified her. "Mama, but I'm scared because Peto looks scary. What if he comes and gets me?"

Fancy rubbed the side of her face. "He's not coming to get you, baby, I promise. Now I need you to lay down in your bed and go back to sleep while I talk to your uncle, Peto. We're going to get that mud and stuff off him so that it stops scaring you. Is that cool?"

Vatican nodded. "But can I leave my night light on?"

"Come on, baby." Fancy picked her up and placed her in the bed. She pulled the covers over her and flipped on the night light so she could have a sense of comfort and security. "Okay, now you're all set." She kissed her lips and gave her a hug. "Sleep well, baby."

"Thank you, mommy."

When Fancy got back to Peto she found him sitting at the kitchen table with her half gallon of Hornitos Brown Liquor. He drank from the bottle, he was in tears. "I fucked up so bad, Fancy. I don't know what is wrong with me. I shouldn't be alive anymore," he cried harder.

"Peto, why don't you tell me exactly what you did. Then I will know how to help you." She placed her hand on his back for support.

"I didn't know that Alexis was Javier's baby. Kelis told me she was mine, but then the baby got dimples like Javier and the same face. But then Kelis said it was my baby, but that was after I screwed up." He pointed at Fancy. "You gotta help me come from under this. It's Javier's fault. All his. If he hadn't fucked my wife, I wouldn't be in this position." He covered his bloodstained face and cried like a baby for five minutes straight. He rocked back and forth feeling sicker and sicker.

Fancy grew impatient. She could only take so much of a grown-ass man sitting in front of her crying like a child. She slapped her hand on the table. "Enough! Now stop all this pussyfooting and tell me what you've done, Peto! Now!"

Peto's eyes went blank. "I killed Alexis, then I killed Kelis, and it's Javier's fuckin' fault, not mine." He scooted his chair back and stood up. He grabbed a box of leftover KFC chicken out of the refrigerator and began eating it cold like a savage.

Fancy was stunned, and suddenly she felt unsafe for herself and Vatican. "Peto, I don't know what to say. I mean that was your family. Why would you do such a thing?"

He cried with a mouthful of food. "I don't know, I'm so sorry!" he wailed, the mashed chicken falling out of his mouth and to the floor.

Fancy got up and looked down the hall toward Vatican's door. "So why are you here, right now? What do you want from me?"

"You're going to help me catch, Javier. Then I am going to kill him. It's as simple as that."

***

Javier turned Finesse around in a circle and dipped her. They'd been slow dancing in front of the fireplace for a full hour and to Javier, it felt like only minutes. He pulled Finesse back up and held her close to his body. "This was one of the things my father did with my mother when we were little that I really admired. I think there is nothing more romantic than when two people care about each other they dance and be intimate in such a way." He turned her around again and pulled her back to him.

Finesse laughed. "You know for a Playboy Javier you speak to me in many terms that could be misconstrued as if you are seeing something long term with me."

Javier brushed his lips against her soft skin. "On some real shit, I like you a lot already. I would love to establish something long term with you."

Finesse eased out of his embrace and walked in front of the roaring fire. "Javier, you don't even know me. How could you see anything long term when we haven't even known each other more than a week? That makes no sense."

Javier came behind her and wrapped his arms around her waist. "My grandparents have been married for fifty years happily. For them, it was love at first sight. They married within a month of knowing each other. When I asked them how did they know the other was the one, they both said, you will know when you know."

"You will know when you know. What does that mean?"

Javier kissed her neck. "From the moment you stepped foot in front of me, I knew. Man, you're so alluring, Finesse. I have never in my life seen such beauty. I am weak around you and my heart bleeds warmly. Man, I didn't even know I had a heart until I laid eyes on you."

Finesse closed her eyes. "I'm not all that, Javier. My whole life people have teased me because I was so black, and my hair was so kinky. They treated me like filth which is why I worked so hard in school. When I hear you call me beautiful it seems so far-fetched that I want to call you a liar. I hate that you make me feel so good. You are getting under my skin, and I'm a very closed off girl." She was having a hard time playing her role now. The worlds of fiction and reality were playing tricks on her.

Javier turned her around so that they were forehead to forehead. "I am not a good person. I am a drug lord, and a womanizer. I live for the countless bundles of cash, the fast life and everything that comes along with it. But I swear to you on the next breath of my father Rodolfo Peralta that I will slow down for you. I will tune in to the world that is you, Finesse. You make me feel weak and strong at the same time. You make me feel evil and religious together. I want you, and I will do whatever it takes to get you to be my woman. Just tell me your price for love."

Finesse slid her arms around his neck and kissed his lips. "Stop talking to me like that. You don't know what that's doing to me." She kissed him again.

Javier grabbed her ass and squeezed it. "I speak from my heart. I'm crazy about you, I need you Finesse." He bit into her neck and picked her up.

Finesse moaned the first thought that came to her mind was fuck the Agency. They would be there when she finished with Javier, besides this date night was off the books. Sure, she would have to report it, but the specifics weren't important. She would omit the part where she put the pussy on him. She snickered.

Javier laid her down on the big bed and pulled her sundress back. He licked all over the front of her white panties until her chocolate lips were visible through the fabric. Once they were, he pulled the material to the side and groaned deep within his throat. He could smell her; it drove him insane.

Finesse pushed him away and crawled to all fours. It had been a long time since she'd gotten any trim. She slapped her ass and made it jiggle in front of Javier. "Come and get it, Daddy."

Javier ripped the buttons of his Polo shirts undoing them. He got behind Finesse and slid home with one stroke. He whimpered, she was so hot and wet, and he was so riled up. He pulled back, and slammed home for the second time and came.

Finesse was none the wiser. She knew she was wrong for fucking the man that her Agency was investigating but being wrong at the moment felt so right. She took a hold of the bed and fucked back into Javier's lap over and over.

"Unnhhh! Unnhhh! Unnhhh! Daddy! Get it, Daddy! Shit!" She closed her eyes and geeked on his piece.

Javier grew harder. He took a hold of her hips and pulled her back to him while he dug her out loving her feel. "I love this pussy! I love this pussy! Shit Finesse!" He roared and couldn't help cumming again.

Finesse scrunched her face and came smashing back into him. "Fuck, Javier!" She slowly twerked on his dick milking him, then she fell on the bed breathing hard with him on top of her back. 'What the fuck have I gotten myself into,' she thought.

Chapter 17

Joaquin kneeled beside the bed where Emilia was still sleeping and looked her over. Her hair was all over her face. There was cold in one of her eyes, and during the mid-morning hours, she'd managed to have just a tidbit of slob dry in the corner of her mouth. She slept with a frown on her face, and he found her so attractive and alluring that he couldn't take his eyes off her. He placed his left hand on her face and held it there. His thumb brushed over her lips. She was perfect.

Emilia slowly opened her eyes at the feel of Joaquin stroking her face. "Joaquin, Papi, what time is it?" She stretched her toes, and arms in different directions.

"It's ten in the morning, you were obviously tired. How are you feeling?" He moved a bit of her curly hair out of her face.

"Like you said, I am feeling quite tired. I don't know why." She licked her lips and wiped the slob from her face. "Were you looking at me as I slept so rough? What's the matter with you?" She sat up and began to clean the cold out of her eye.

Joaquin sat on the bed beside her. "Emilia, tongue you are so fine that I can't believe it. All these years you and I have been best friends. I have never taken the time to actually look at you. I guess the way that I was supposed to. Now that I am, I feel confident saying you are the most beautiful girl in all the world. Despite your bad attitude of course."

"Bad attitude?" She frowned at Joaquin. "I don't have a bad attitude. And how can you build me up on one side and then come right back around and take my joy away from me by saying I have a bad attitude. I thought you loved me?" She poked out her bottom lip and crossed her arms in front of her chest.

Joaquin wasted little time. He leaned over and sucked it into his mouth. "Gimme that lip," he growled like a Lion.

"No." Emilia turned her head. She could taste that her breath wasn't fresh, and she was extremely apprehensive about Joaquin smelling it. "Let me brush first, Joaquin. I feel so self-conscious."

"What? Oh, now I really gotta have some of that tongue. He hopped all the way on the bed, and straddled her, taking her wrists and pinning them to the bed. "Gimme my kisses, Emilia. "

"No, get off me, Joaquin. I need to brush my teeth first. You know how I am," she said this with her face turned to the side, and through clenched teeth to prevent any odor from seeping out of her mouth.

Joaquin kissed all over her face. "You're my baby, and there is nothin' that comes from you that I wouldn't love, including your morning breath. Now give me my kisses." He continued to kiss all over her face, he wound up on her neck biting and sucking.

Emilia felt herself becoming aroused. "Joaquin, brushing my teeth will only take two minutes. Can't you allow it?"

Joaquin shook his head. "True love doesn't hide its flaws. You are perfect for me. Your breath as well. Now stop playing and let me love you."

Emilia ceased her struggling and turned on her back in submission. She looked up at Joaquin with her hair all over her pillow. "Kiss me, Joaquin. Kiss me and tell me how much you love me while you do it." She slid her arms into the crux of his neck.

Joaquin lowered himself downward until his muscular chest was against hers. "I love you, Emilia. There has never been a more perfect girl in this world for me more than you. You are priceless." He kissed her lips and sucked all over

138

them. His tongue slowly slid into her mouth, their tongues danced. He sucked on hers and began breathing hard.

"I love you so much, Joaquin. I have always loved you." More kissing. "You make me feel like a Goddess. I feel so perfect, and it's because of you. Even though I know, I am not." She kissed him some more and pulled him all the way down until he was lying between her thighs. Her sky-blue nightgown fell backward. Her thick thighs were wide open. She felt aroused, and hungry for him.

Joaquin stopped and gazed into her eyes. "You are perfect. Everything about you is perfect, Emilia. There should be no wonder why I love you so crazy the way that I do. You are my strength and my completion. I know without a shadow of a doubt that I will be in love with you until my last dying day.

Emilia flipped Joaquin over so that she was straddling him. She placed her hands on his chest. From this angle, she looked like a wild Goddess with her waist-length hair all over her. She leaned down and kissed his lips. "Joaquin, I know we talked about waiting until our wedding night, but I need you, right now. The space in between my legs is calling for you. I'm so wet." She ground her pussy into his piece that began hardening as soon as she straddled him.

Joaquin took ahold of her waist and trailed his hands all over her naked thighs. They were juicy. He didn't stop until he got to her perfect feet, with the small manicured toes. "But we agreed that our relationship would be different from the others that we have been in. This one should be about more than sex. What happened to that?"

Emilia rolled off him and laid beside him. She pulled up her gown and opened her thighs again. She pulled her panties to the side to show him her pussy. Using two fingers she opened the lips. "Can you see how wet you make me, Joaquin? Do you see how my pinkness is a rosy color?"

Joaquin began to shake. "Yeah."

"That's because I am horny for my best friend." She rubbed her cat and sliced the lips with her middle finger. "Do you remember when we were little, and our mothers used to wash us in the same tub?" She continued to touch herself.

Joaquin couldn't take his eyes off her. "I remember."

"Do you remember how you used to poke at this right here because you were wondering why it didn't look like yours? It was so naked and smooth like it is now. Remember how you used to ask me to let you touch it, but I was so scared, and your little thing would be standing up because of seeing this?"

Joaquin's piece was jumping like crazy. He thought back to when they were little, he couldn't wait for bath time so he could see Emilia's naked parts. Whenever their parents left them alone, he would try to find all kinds of ways to get her to expose herself to him, or to allow him to touch her. He could smell a hint of her sex and it was driving him crazy. "I remember."

Emilia rubbed her finger around the lips of her pussy, then she wiped it on his lips. "Remember you used to love when I did that?"

Joaquin's dick was so hard now that it hurt. It was sticking up against Emilia's butt. "Emilia you're driving me crazy."

She leaned down and brushed her lips against his. "Everything you wanted to do to that little kitty back then you can do now. It's hot for you, Joaquin. It's always supposed to have been for you. Now you can play with it as much as you want. We can go back to the tub, Joaquin." She licked all over his lips and pressed her ass backward until she could feel his pole. Its length was a bit intimidating for her, but he was Joaquin, she would figure it out.

Joaquin slid his hands under her gown and took ahold of her naked ass cheeks. He gripped them and rubbed all over them. Her heart called out to him. "Emilia I want you, baby. I want you so bad that it's driving me crazy."

Emilia bit into his neck and sucked hard. She lowered her body and planted bites and kisses all over his neck, and chest. When she got to his abs, she licked all over the ridges. Her fingers played over the muscles there. She licked southward until she came to the waistband of his boxers. She pulled them down. His dick sprung up like a dark brown cucumber. She wrapped her fingers around the wide base and began to stroke him. He was huge.

Emilia shivered. "It was never this big, I guess we aren't kids anymore.

Joaquin reached over her back and pulled her gown up. He wanted to see how her panties looked stuck in between her ass cheek. The sight made him whimper. Both of Emilia's cara-mel cheeks were split by her underwear. They were jiggling, with a few light stretch marks across them. She was thick. Joaquin slapped her on the ass and squeezed it.

Emilia turned all the way around so that her ass was facing him. She backed up and continued to stroke Joaquin mildly. She squeezed his dick and kissed the head. "This is mine, Joaquin. You belong to me now. I'm not gon' play about you, and you shouldn't expect me to." She licked all around his head, then sucked him into her mouth taking him halfway down.

Joaquin pulled her backward. Her gown came down around his head. He made her sit on his mouth. As soon as she did his tongue began to swipe and lick all over her pussy. Her sex lips opened like the petals of a rose. He inhaled her deeply and pulled her down further. Her wetness smeared across his cheek. His tongue slipped into her slit and reached as far as it could. He was thirsty for her taste, and her cum. He closed his eyes and imagined their bath times when they were little. He saw her kitty back then in his mind's eye, and he remembered how much he craved her. He began to shake and shiver.

Emilia sucked him with her jaws hollowing in and out. She arched her back and moaned at the feel of him peeling her lips open and licking around her clitoris. She wanted him so bad. She needed him. "Joaquin, shouldn't we?" She sucked him faster and harder. A loud slurping noise came from her mouth and his piece.

Joaquin rubbed his face all over her middle. He trapped her clitoris with his lips and sucked. His tongue flicked faster and faster. Her juices ran onto his cheeks and leaked into his ear canal. He kept licking. He held her to him and went into overdrive.

Emilia had her eyes closed while she pumped Joaquin. She backed into his lips and trembled. "Aw shit, Papi! Papi! I'm cumming! I'm cumming!" she whimpered and came all over him.

Joaquin slid from under her and flipped her over onto her back. He pressed her knees to her shoulders and licked all over her groove. He sucked first her left sex lip, then the right one. He peeled them back and attacked her clitoris. "You're my baby. Arrgh, I'ma kill for you. Cum for me again." He slid his tongue as far into her as it would go and ran in and out until she came again screaming how much she loved him. Her pussy began to squirt all over his face. He snickered and kissed her lips individually.

Emilia couldn't breathe. She opened her mouth wide and inhaled as hard as she could, to take in some oxygen. Her tongue ran all over her lips. Her pussy jumped. Her nipples were so hard that they stood out from her breasts a full inch.

Joaquin rubbed her box, it was flaming hot. He played with the lips, and sucked his fingers into his mouth, before playing with them some more. "It's almost time for us to raid the Governor's mansion. We have to get the attention of the politicians in Puerto Rico. Mayor Cruz will continue to dismiss our people unless we show her that we are ready for war." He ran his thumb around her clitoris while she slowly humped into it.

Emilia pulled him down to her and positioned him between her thighs. His big dick beat against her wet lips. "You mean to tell me this is what's going through your head? When I got all this pussy between my legs. Are you serious?" She squeezed his piece and ran his head up and down inside of her slit.

Joaquin closed his eyes and nearly fell on top of her. "Emilia, you're giving me all I can handle. Please, baby, if we wait just imagine how special our wedding night will be."

Emilia allowed his dick head to slide into her for a few inches and then she pulled it back out. "Are you sure?"

The cool air hit the moisture that was around his piece caused by her juices and Joaquin began to shake. "Yes." He wanted things to be different with Emilia. When they laid down the first time and went all the way, he wanted them to do it as husband and wife the way that the Elders of La Perla had intended for it to be.

He took his dick from her hand and kissed her lips. "You know that a man really loves you when he is willing to wait to enter you. There is no rush, I plan on being with you for a lifetime."

Emilia sat up and pulled him back down on top of her. "Then I want to get married twice. Once we will do just for the paperwork and by a courthouse, and the second time will be a glorious wedding after we get our point across in San Juan. How does that sound?"

Joaquin ran his hand between her thighs and cuffed her box. "It sounds like I'ma be getting some of this more sooner than I thought."

"You damn right, Papi. Now let me get you off like you just did me."

Joaquin flipped on to his back happily. "What a wife to be."

Chapter 18

Having Finesse as inspiration, Javier went into hustling over-drive with his crew of dope and corner boys. In thirty days he was able to gross his first million dollars. Funds that he felt, he'd made without Rodolfo being over his shoulder and directing him at every turn. He was proud of himself, and instead of spending the proceeds on frivolous materialistic things he decided to take the million dollars and invest it right back into the game. Using new connections out of Mexico, he was able to purchase a million-dollars-worth of product after the first month, and the Sinaloa Cartel fronted him another million at a five percent interest rate that Javier found fair. Javier took the two-million in product and flipped it in sixty days by flooding the streets of Miami and bullying his way into the game of Atlanta where the LGBTQ community at first had a stranglehold on the narcotics world. Javier had other things in mind.

In the second month of his dealings with the Sinaloa Cartel, and after he was fronted the additional million-dollars-worth of Tar and Coke from the Cartel Bosses south of the border, Javier put together a deadly hit squad of lethal savages that were dead set on crushing all other kingpins, and trap stars that operated out of Atlanta Georgia. He sent his men into Atlanta with one mission: to assassinate all the top bosses in the city and get back out and lay low in Boston where he had arranged for safe houses while the one-month killing spree ensued.

Javier began to study geographical maps and adopt points of attack for each rival until slowly but surely, they started to be vanquished sometimes two or three in a day. When the boss for a certain crew or cartel was crushed, Javier moved his Peralta Dope Boys into their spaces, and gradually took over their clientele with topnotch narcotics. Atlanta was a new market for him, and when he coupled it with the steady flow of cash coming from the state of Florida, he began to see incredible numbers that even he couldn't believe.

In the third month of Javier's new endeavors, Rodolfo flew back from the Dominican Republic to meet with his son. He woke Javier up early one Sunday morning by ringing the doorbell to his red-bricked home. Rodolfo adjusted his cufflinks and checked the time of his Rolex watch when two armed Savages slowly slid behind him. All he saw were the shadows of the two bandits. He turned around and was met with their masked faces.

Javier appeared from around the corner of the building. He was dressed in a white Gucci robe and was still wearing his house slippers. "Papi, what brings you here? I thought you were in the Dominican Republic?" He stepped before Rodolfo with a sly smile on his face. He'd tooted two lines of pink cocaine and was feeling riled up. He pulled his nose and swallowed the drip that was taking place in the back of his throat.

Rodolfo saw that his son was trying to show off in front of him by his set up and wasn't amused. "We need to talk, Javier, right now. Open this door." He mugged the bandits behind him and looked over to Javier when they didn't move.

Javier rubbed the hairs on his chin. "So, let me get his straight, you've flown back early all the way from the Dominican Republic because you needed to talk to me?" Javier clicked his tongue on his teeth. "This can't be good. Should I be worried?" He gave his henchmen the eye for them to back away from Rodolfo. They did.

"We can't discuss what I want to discuss out here in front of the world. We need to be in private quarters. Now open the door, and let's go inside," Rodolfo demanded. He felt himself becoming heated. He began to sweat.

Javier opened the front door and pushed it inward. Come inside, Pop. Tell me what's on your mind?"

Rodolfo stormed inside and headed right into Javier's den. Once inside he poured him a glass of Scotch and downed it. "Javier get your ass here son. You're really pissing me off."

"Well, you know what they say, it's better to be pissed off than pissed on. I mean unless you are into that sort of thing." He snickered. "What can I do for you my seed bearer?"

Rodolfo broke the glass on the floor and pointed at Javier. "You son of a bitch! How dare you take five hundred thousand dollars from me to connect with those Mexican bastards down south. Do you have any idea what you have gotten yourself into? This family? My God, Javier. We are in some deep shit, right now."

Javier took two Percocets out of his robe pocket and popped them. He chased the pills with a glass of Patron. "I meant to replace that money. That's my bad." He walked to the back of the den and rolled beside the fold in the closet door. He grabbed a duffel bag and dropped it at Rodolfo's feet. This one has a million dollars in cash. That's a hundred percent profit on your end. Now get the fuck off my back." He mugged him.

Rodolfo side-eyed him. He couldn't believe that there were a million dollars in the bag before him. He kneeled to one knee and unzipped it. He ran his hand through a bunch of hundred-dollar bills. He pulled out a stack of them and looked it over. "Where did you get this?"

Javier was busy drinking the Patron from the bottle. He stopped and burped. "From the streets, I only used your lil' cash to get a leg up in the game. Now that I'm rocking and rolling, I don't need shit from you no more."

"Oh, so now you think you are some big shot because you made a million dollars? Do you have any idea how crazy things are about to get for you? Once you cross the threshold of a million in this game that's when all the real sharks come at you. That's when people that are high up start paying attention. When they have their eyes on you there is nothing you can do but strategize every single day in order to stay alive. You are involved with the Sinaloa's now. They hate our people. They will use you up as much as they can before they annihilate you. What part of that don't you understand?"

"Oh, I understand every part of that. What you don't understand is that if a mafucka wanna come and mess with mine then they have to be ready to go to war and turn the streets red with blood. I am Javier Peralta, fuck the Sinaloa Cartel. I am officially announcing that I will head the Peralta Cartel. I'm done with chasing behind you in order to get your approval. I'm done depending on any man other than myself. I am disconnecting myself from you Rodolfo and I am allowing you to continue to find your favorite son, Joaquin that is down in La Perla."

"Finding Joaquin, what are you talking about?"

Javier laughed. "You're an old man. You're not so good with technology, and your password for everything is either Martina or Joaquin." He stepped into his father's face. "I read what you put inside your digital journal. You set up some of your buyers down in Puerto Rico so that they could be robbed by Joaquin. You gave that muthafucka a million dollars and all that dope and you come down on me for taking five hundred thousand in order to further our family's enterprises? How dare you, Rodolfo?"

Rodolfo was shocked that Javier had uncovered so much. He became angry. "You stole from me Javier, and I didn't give your brother anything. He took what he needed from those sons of a bitches in La Perla. It serves them right for causing so much havoc. That government wants to get rid of our

148

people down there. They want to vanquish us all, and your brother Joaquin is the only hope that they will be unsuccessful. Should I have assisted him covertly?"

"You always loved your precious, Joaquin. Justina and Martina as well. You never gave a care about your illegitimate son. Had Martina never refused to leave Puerto Rico after the hurricane I am sure you would have never thought to get close to me. You only did it because of your own guilty conscience. Shame on you, Rodolfo. And you know what, thank you. Thank you for helping me become a man."

"You're not a man, Javier. You're a misguided child with hatred in your heart for your loved ones. Nothing good will come from that."

Javier pressed his forehead to Rodolfo's. Four of his bloodthirsty savages came out of the hallway and stood behind him. "I am a man. And when it comes to Martina, Justina, and Joaquin, fuck them! Do you hear me? Fuck them! Not only am I taking over the Peralta throne, I am going to crush Joaquin just like I've been crushing every other rival on the Southeast coast. I will stand atop of the totem pole alone. Fuck you, and fuck everybody else that honors your name."

Rodolfo couldn't believe he was experiencing such rebellion from Javier. It hurt his heart. Ever since Javier was a little boy, he'd tried his best to give him the world. "If this is how you feel then you are disowned. Good luck with your cartel. You do not have my blessing. It will go to Joaquin." Rodolfo backed away from him and walked out of his home.

Javier laughed and felt the ice coming over his heart. He would prove to Rodolfo that he was the true head of the family. He would find Joaquin and smash him like a cockroach. He would make his younger brother pay for the transgressions of his father. He hated Joaquin, and he hated Martina. The verdict of Justina was yet to be decided, but he was sure he would hate her, too. He smiled, he imagined making her pay in a more unconventional way, she was so beautiful. He stepped to the window and pulled back the curtain to his home. He watched his father get into his Bentley and pull out of the driveway.

Joaquin turned to his men. "Tonight, we have our first true meeting to announce my new position as head of the Peralta Cartel."

***

Finesse laid out the last of the fifteen pictures along the table for Javier to see. "Okay, now you need to pay close attention to this power player, right here because he is the Drug Lords that will be looking to come at you from all angles. This older, heavy-set fellow's name is Juan Salazar. He is head of the New Orleans Syndicate. He runs military assault rifles all the way from China back to the United States. He is also connected with the Columbians, and the Sinaloas out of Sinaloa Mexico. He is a ruthless, and cold-hearted individual with no regard for human life other than his own. You must be conscious of him and his crew of like-minded callous individuals at all times." She placed her hand on his shoulder while she kept her eyes pinned on the pictures before them.

"How do you know all of this?" Javier picked up Juan's picture and zoomed into the man's evil eyes.

"Just like there are a lot of things I don't know about you, but I give you the benefit of the doubt, you must do the same thing with me. You have to trust me. Just know that I have your best interests at heart." She sighed and wished what she was saying about his interests were true. Over the past few months, she'd become quite fond of Javier. He tugged on her heartstrings and made her feel special, that was something she didn't think any man was capable of doing.

Javier looked her over. "I do trust you, and I'ma take heed to everything you are telling me. Now walk me through all this one more time and break down the connections that report back to Sinaloa. This shit seems like it's really interesting."

"Okay, now if you—" She stopped mid-sentence because there was a knock at the door.

Javier stood up and held up a finger. "Hold on, I already know who this is because I only gave my security permission to let my lil' cousin Peto come through. Let me holler at him real quick. I'll be right back, baby." He leaned over and kissed her lips.

"Mmm, hurry back, Honey. We need to get this figured out before you make your next major move." The more moves Javier made up the Narcotics ladder meant the more powerful of a bust she would have when she made it. She could already see the tabloids.

"A'ight, hold on." Javier grabbed his .40 Glock off the table and went and opened the door after seeing Peto standing outside of it. "What's up lil' cuz, what did you need to holler at me about that was so important?"

Peto looked both ways. He felt his heart beating hard in his chest. It all was all or nothing. He took a step back and pulled two twin Desert Eagles from his belt. "You took my family away from me! Die Javier!" Then his fingers were squeezing the triggers.

151

Chapter 19

Joaquin jumped out of his Cadillac Escalade and came around the big body of the truck. He stopped in front of Emilia's passenger's door and pulled it open. She stepped out of the truck in a form-fitting white Gucci dress that Joaquin had bought for her only hours later. Joaquin held out his hand and took a hold of hers. Together they marched into the courthouse with sixty of La Perla's loyal savages behind them. Emilia's hair flowed lovely over her shoulders. She looked up to Joaquin and felt butterflies taking over her stomach.

Joaquin held open the door and allowed her to walk in before him. Once inside the church, Father Juarez was already awaiting their arrival. Joaquin led the way and stopped in front of Father Juarez. He turned to Emilia and held her hands. Their savages settled into the pews of the church. The sounds of their shoes squeaking, and clothes rustling as they situated themselves were noticeable in the church.

Joaquin stroked Emilia's cheek. He spoke to her in Spanish. "Baby, you already know we are going to do this the right way when the time presents itself, right?" He looked into her sparkling eyes and smiled.

She nodded. "As long as you are going to be my husband, Joaquin, that is all that matters to me. I love you so much."

Joaquin felt his eyes become watery. He took a deep breath and blew it out. "Father marry us."

Father Juarez stepped forward and blessed Joaquin, then Emilia. He uttered a few verses from the Bible, then he began to go through the ceremony of marrying the two. After ten minutes of the formalities, he finally came to the part that Joaquin was used to hearing. "Emilia Jimenez, do you take Joaquin Peralta as your husband? Will you promise to love him through sickness and in health, for richer or for poor, will you obey him, and stand as his wife for as long as you shall live?"

Emilia nodded her head. "With all that I am, I will." She slid the gold ring on to Joaquin's finger.

"And Joaquin Peralta, do you take Emilia Jimenez as your wife? Will you love her, will you cherish her, will you provide for her, and be there by her side through sickness and in health, for richer and for poor, as long as you both shall live?"

"I promise to do all these things and so much more. She is the light of my life." He slid the one-carat diamond ring upon her finger and kissed the back of her hand.

Father Juarez held up his hands and did the crucifix over the pair. "Then it brings me great joy to say that by the powers that are in me, and by the grace of Jesus Christ I now pronounce you husband and wife. Joaquin, you may kiss your lovely Bride."

Joaquin picked Emilia up into the air and allowed her to wrap her thighs around him. He kissed her lips, and seconds later they were tonguing each other down hungrily. The church erupted with applause before the savages hopped up and back on point. Joaquin set Emilia down and looked into her eyes happily. "I love you, Baby. I promise to be the best man for you."

"I trust you, Joaquin. I trust you with all my life." She wrapped her arms around his neck and kissed his lips again. Emilia had never been so happy in all her life. She was wishing that her mother had been there in order to see her and Joaquin wed, or at least Cecilia. But she was thankful for the moment just the same.

***

Later that night Joaquin held hands with Emilia while they walked barefoot in the sand along the beach. The waves of the water crashed into the big rocks loudly. It was a hot and humid day. There was a breeze coming off the East that gave the pair a sense of relief. Emilia's hair blew in the dry wind. She looked over and up to Joaquin pulling a strand of hair out of her face.

"Ever since I was a little girl, Joaquin, I've had a crazy crush on you. I was too shy to act on it, but I always said that when I get older I was going to marry you. Now look and behold I've done it. I am officially a Peralta. It's time to get down to business."

Joaquin laughed. "I don't even know what that means, but I used to say the same thing as well. I always said that when I grew up I was going to marry you and that we were going to have a big house. Now that I have you as my wife, I have accomplished that part. Now I need to get you the house and the security that you deserve as a woman. Then I want to start putting some babies right in there." He rubbed her stomach.

Emilia smacked his hand away. "I hope you don't think I am ready to lay down and start having kids because I am nowhere near that. I am ready to get on the front lines and fight for the land of La Perla. This is my home, and if my husband is going to be the King of this island then I am going to be equally as important. It is my birthright."

Joaquin stopped in his tracks. "Emilia, don't talk so stupidly. You are a wife now. Why would I allow you to fight in a man's war? You are supposed to be protected and at home. I will do the heavy lifting, and I will stand as a knight over La Perla."

Emilia had to double-take before she made sure that Joaquin was standing in front of her and talking the way that he was. She turned her head sideways and jerked it backward.

"If you think that just because I have become your wife it means you can control or muffle me then you have me sadly mistaken. I am a woman. I am strong. I am determined to fight for La Perla. I refuse to be denied the opportunity to defend my country. I will not allow the establishment to silence me, nor will I allow my husband to do so. Do you understand me?"

Joaquin clenched his jaw and tensed his muscles. He looked angrily into Emilia's face for a brief moment, then he became soft for her. "You are going to drive me into an early grave, Emilia." He held her chin and rubbed the side of her face with his thumb. "I would never look to silence, nor prevent you from fighting for La Perla. I married you because I see myself inside of you more than anyone else in this world.

"Nobody loves La Perla more than you and I." He sighed. "Emilia, you are my wife now, which means we are one flesh and one spirit. We are equal. All that I can build for the sake of our people you can build also. But you are responsible for building it up and fighting from a feminine standpoint. Build up your army of female warriors that are willing to put it all on the line and die for the sake of our land that is La Perla. I believe in you, and I will always have your back. With your lil' feisty self." He pressed his lips to her forehead.

She closed her eyes and smiled. "Thank you for believing in me, Papi. I thought for a minute I was going to have to get all up in your butt. Though we are people of tradition I do not desire to be stifled like the women before. I will submit to you out of love, not tradition and fear, and you are supposed to do the same. Also, even though we are Warriors I still think that it is essential that we come fully under God. We are going to need that added protection."

"You just thought all of this through thoroughly, huh?"

"Yeah, so what do you say?" She placed her small hands on his chest.

"I'm willing to do whatever it takes to make you happy. You are my life, Emilia." He pulled her to him and held her close.

***

Martina opened the oven door to her stove and pulled out the pan of baked chicken. She slid it onto the stove and fanned away the smoke. She danced to the music coming out of the speakers of her old school, small radio. She turned in a circle and slid across the floor. She laughed, she could feel her lower back paining her. She placed her hand on it to give her a sense of relief. "Whew. Where did the years go?" She spoke loudly to herself in Spanish.

Pedro stepped into the kitchen with an evil sneer on his face. He eyed Martina with hatred. He took a serrated blade out of the sheath of his knife case. Before becoming a proud member of the San Juan Jackers Pedro's initiation included murdering the household of Joaquin. Due to a severed tongue as a motive to cross over to the Jackers and to complete the tasks that they requested, Pedro was ready to start with Martina.

'I have to get me a dog or something,' she thought. 'This is the second time somebody has crept up on me.' "To what do I owe this surprise, Pedro?"

Pedro couldn't talk, and even if he could he wasn't in the mood to do so. He flipped the kitchen table and grabbed a hold of Martina. Before she could fight him back, he brought the knife down into her back and twisted it, pulled it out and slammed it into her again. He knocked her to the floor and straddled her body. Then he started stabbing over and over with no regard.

Justina heard the flipping of the table and it woke her out of her sleep. She ran her hand over her face and yawned, stretching her legs out. She rubbed her stomach and slipped out of the bed neglecting to throw a robe around her Bra and panties. She yawned again and came to the bedroom door and stopped to pull her panties out of her butt. The hefty cheeks had swallowed them. She opened the bedroom door and stepped out of it. She sleepily walked down the hallway with her eyes closed, every few steps she would open them to see what was in front of her. She popped them wide open when she got close to the kitchen and heard Pedro grunting loudly while he stabbed Martina's lifeless body over and over for his own amusement. Justina stopped in her tracks when the scene registered in her brain. She screamed.

"Oh, my God! What are you doing to my mother?" She hollered.

Pedro stood up and wiped the blade off on Martina's cheek. He looked over Justina's perfect body and became lustful. He stepped over Martina. Justina slowly took in the scene before her eyes, then took off in the other direction. Pedro stood still just glaring at Justina. Then suddenly he took off after her.

***

Joaquin led Emilia back to the Escalade and helped her get inside of it. He closed the passenger's door behind her and walked around to get into the driver's seat of the truck when six black Hummers rolled into the parking lot and stopped in front of him and his crew of savages. Joaquin's men upped their firearms ready to crush whoever was inside of the Military vehicles. Joaquin stood at the ready, fearless. Emilia hopped out with both .9 millimeters in her hands ready to die beside Joaquin of the mission called for it.

The lead Hummer's door opened, and Sudan stepped out of it with black war paint all over her face. Her animals came behind her with military issued assault rifles. She held up her hand to keep them at bay. Then she stepped up to Joaquin and lowered her eyes. "Are you willing to die for La Perla tonight?" As she finished the words six more Hummers rolled into the lot, and the masked Sudanese killers hopped out of them heavily armed. "If you aren't really ready to die for this land, bow down. Now!" she hollered.

To Be Continued...
Dope Gods 2
Coming Soon

Submission Guideline

Submit the first three chapters of your completed manuscript to ldpsubmissions@gmail.com, subject line: Your book's title. The manuscript must be in a .doc file and sent as an attachment. Document should be in Times New Roman, double spaced and in size 12 font. Also, provide your synopsis and full contact information. If sending multiple submissions, they must each be in a separate email.

Have a story but no way to send it electronically? You can still submit to LDP/Ca$h Presents. Send in the first three chapters, written or typed, of your completed manuscript to:

LDP: Submissions Dept
Po Box 870494
Mesquite, Tx 75187

DO NOT send original manuscript. Must be a duplicate.

Provide your synopsis and a cover letter containing your full contact information.

Thanks for considering LDP and Ca$h Presents.

<u>Coming Soon from Lock Down Publications/Ca$h Presents</u>

BOW DOWN TO MY GANGSTA

By **Ca$h**

TORN BETWEEN TWO

By **Coffee**

THE STREETS STAINED MY SOUL **II**

By **Marcellus Allen**

BLOOD OF A BOSS **VI**

SHADOWS OF THE GAME II

By **Askari**

LOYAL TO THE GAME **IV**

By **T.J. & Jelissa**

A DOPEBOY'S PRAYER **II**

By **Eddie "Wolf" Lee**

IF LOVING YOU IS WRONG… **III**

By **Jelissa**

TRUE SAVAGE **VII**

MIDNIGHT CARTEL III

DOPE BOY MAGIC III

By **Chris Green**

BLAST FOR ME **III**

A SAVAGE DOPEBOY III

CUTTHROAT MAFIA II

By **Ghost**

A HUSTLER'S DECEIT III

KILL ZONE **II**

Hood Rich

SLAUGHTER GANG IV

RUTHLESS HEART III

By Willie Slaughter

THE HEART OF A SAVAGE III

By Jibril Williams

FUK SHYT II

By Blakk Diamond

THE DOPEMAN'S BODYGAURD II

By Tranay Adams

TRAP GOD II

By Troublesome

YAYO III

A SHOOTER'S AMBITION II

By S. Allen

GHOST MOB

Stilloan Robinson

KINGPIN DREAMS II

By Paper Boi Rari

CREAM

By Yolanda Moore

SON OF A DOPE FIEND II

By Renta

FOREVER GANGSTA II

By Adrian Dulan

LOYALTY AIN'T PROMISED II

By Keith Williams

THE PRICE YOU PAY FOR LOVE II

DOPE GIRL MAGIC II

By Destiny Skai

THE LIFE OF A HOOD STAR

By Rashia Wilson

TOE TAGZ III

By Ah'Million

CONFESSIONS OF A GANGSTA II

By Nicholas Lock

PAID IN KARMA III

By **Meesha**

I'M NOTHING WITHOUT HIS LOVE II

By Monet Dragun

CAUGHT UP IN THE LIFE II

By Robert Baptiste

NEW TO THE GAME II

By **Malik D. Rice**

Life of a Savage II

By **Romell Tukes**

Quiet Money II

By **Trai'Quan**

Available Now

RESTRAINING ORDER **I & II**

By **CA$H & Coffee**

LOVE KNOWS NO BOUNDARIES **I II & III**

Dope Gods

IF LOVING HIM IS WRONG…I & II

LOVE ME EVEN WHEN IT HURTS I II III

By **Jelissa**

WHEN THE STREETS CLAP BACK I & II III

THE HEART OF A SAVAGE I II

By **Jibril Williams**

A DISTINGUISHED THUG STOLE MY HEART I II & III

LOVE SHOULDN'T HURT I II III IV

RENEGADE BOYS I II III IV

PAID IN KARMA I II

By **Meesha**

A GANGSTER'S CODE I &, II III

A GANGSTER'S SYN I II III

THE SAVAGE LIFE I II III

CHAINED TO THE STREETS I II

By J-Blunt

PUSH IT TO THE LIMIT

By **Bre' Hayes**

BLOOD OF A BOSS **I, II, III, IV, V**

SHADOWS OF THE GAME

By **Askari**

THE STREETS BLEED MURDER **I, II & III**

THE HEART OF A GANGSTA I II& III

By **Jerry Jackson**

CUM FOR ME I II III IV V

An **LDP Erotica Collaboration**

BRIDE OF A HUSTLA **I II & II**

Dope Gods

THE FETTI GIRLS **I, II& III**

CORRUPTED BY A GANGSTA I, II III, IV

BLINDED BY HIS LOVE

THE PRICE YOU PAY FOR LOVE

DOPE GIRL MAGIC

By **Destiny Skai**

WHEN A GOOD GIRL GOES BAD

By **Adrienne**

THE COST OF LOYALTY I II

By Kweli

A GANGSTER'S REVENGE **I II III & IV**

THE BOSS MAN'S DAUGHTERS I II III IV V

A SAVAGE LOVE **I & II**

BAE BELONGS TO ME I II

A HUSTLER'S DECEIT I, II, III

WHAT BAD BITCHES DO I, II, III

SOUL OF A MONSTER I II III

KILL ZONE

By **Aryanna**

A KINGPIN'S AMBITON

A KINGPIN'S AMBITION **II**

I MURDER FOR THE DOUGH

By **Ambitious**

TRUE SAVAGE I II III IV V VI

DOPE BOY MAGIC I, II

MIDNIGHT CARTEL I II

By **Chris Green**

Hood Rich

A DOPEBOY'S PRAYER

By **Eddie "Wolf" Lee**

THE KING CARTEL **I, II & III**

By **Frank Gresham**

THESE NIGGAS AIN'T LOYAL **I, II & III**

By **Nikki Tee**

GANGSTA SHYT **I II &III**

By **CATO**

THE ULTIMATE BETRAYAL

By **Phoenix**

BOSS'N UP **I , II & III**

By **Royal Nicole**

I LOVE YOU TO DEATH

By Destiny J

I RIDE FOR MY HITTA

I STILL RIDE FOR MY HITTA

By **Misty Holt**

LOVE & CHASIN' PAPER

By **Qay Crockett**

TO DIE IN VAIN

SINS OF A HUSTLA

By **ASAD**

BROOKLYN HUSTLAZ

By **Boogsy Morina**

BROOKLYN ON LOCK I & II

By **Sonovia**

GANGSTA CITY

Dope Gods

By **Teddy Duke**
A DRUG KING AND HIS DIAMOND I & II III
A DOPEMAN'S RICHES
HER MAN, MINE'S TOO I, II
CASH MONEY HO'S
By Nicole Goosby
TRAPHOUSE KING **I II & III**
KINGPIN KILLAZ I II III
STREET KINGS I II
PAID IN BLOOD **I II**
CARTEL KILLAZ I II III
DOPE GODS
By **Hood Rich**
LIPSTICK KILLAH **I, II, III**
CRIME OF PASSION I II & III
By **Mimi**
STEADY MOBBN' **I, II, III**
THE STREETS STAINED MY SOUL
By **Marcellus Allen**
WHO SHOT YA **I, II, III**
SON OF A DOPE FIEND
Renta
GORILLAZ IN THE BAY **I II III IV**
TEARS OF A GANGSTA
DE'KARI
TRIGGADALE I II
Elijah R. Freeman

Hood Rich

GOD BLESS THE TRAPPERS I, II, III

THESE SCANDALOUS STREETS I, II, III

FEAR MY GANGSTA I, II, III

THESE STREETS DON'T LOVE NOBODY I, II

BURY ME A G I, II, III, IV, V

A GANGSTA'S EMPIRE I, II, III, IV

THE DOPEMAN'S BODYGAURD

Tranay Adams

THE STREETS ARE CALLING

Duquie Wilson

MARRIED TO A BOSS... I II III

By Destiny Skai & Chris Green

KINGZ OF THE GAME I II III IV

Playa Ray

SLAUGHTER GANG I II III

RUTHLESS HEART I II

By Willie Slaughter

FUK SHYT

By Blakk Diamond

DON'T F#CK WITH MY HEART I II

By Linnea

ADDICTED TO THE DRAMA I II III

By Jamila

YAYO I II

A SHOOTER'S AMBITION

By S. Allen

TRAP GOD

Dope Gods

By Troublesome

FOREVER GANGSTA

By Adrian Dulan

TOE TAGZ I II

By Ah'Million

KINGPIN DREAMS

By Paper Boi Rari

CONFESSIONS OF A GANGSTA

By Nicholas Lock

I'M NOTHING WITHOUT HIS LOVE

By Monet Dragun

CAUGHT UP IN THE LIFE

By Robert Baptiste

NEW TO THE GAME

By **Malik D. Rice**

Life of a Savage

By **Romell Tukes**

LOYALTY AIN'T PROMISED

By Keith Williams

Quiet Money

By **Trai'Quan**

<u>BOOKS BY LDP'S CEO, CA$H</u>

<u>TRUST IN NO MAN</u>
<u>TRUST IN NO MAN 2</u>
<u>TRUST IN NO MAN 3</u>
<u>BONDED BY BLOOD</u>
<u>SHORTY GOT A THUG</u>
<u>THUGS CRY</u>
<u>THUGS CRY 2</u>
<u>THUGS CRY 3</u>
<u>TRUST NO BITCH</u>
<u>TRUST NO BITCH 2</u>
<u>TRUST NO BITCH 3</u>
<u>TIL MY CASKET DROPS</u>
<u>RESTRAINING ORDER</u>
<u>RESTRAINING ORDER 2</u>
<u>IN LOVE WITH A CONVICT</u>

<u>Coming Soon</u>
BONDED BY BLOOD 2
BOW DOWN TO MY GANGSTA

Dope Gods